Clean Breaks

Practice Perfect, Book 3

Ruby Lang

Adams Media

New York London Toronto Sydney New Delhi

CRIMSON

Crimson Romance
An Imprint of Simon & Schuster, Inc.
1230 Avenue of the Americas
New York, NY 10020

ISBN 1-5072-0392-6
ISBN 978-1-5072-0391-0 (ebook)

CHAPTER ONE

"Sarah, that guy is looking at you."

Sarah Soon, obstetrician/gynecologist, maker of lists, taker of names, kicker of asses, put down her beer and gave her hair a flip.

"Which guy?"

"The Asian guy over there. The one with the"— her friend Petra made a cupping motion—"the physique."

Sarah turned right around—she didn't do subtle—and took in a good eyeful of the long body hugged lovingly by a gray t-shirt and jeans. She noted the square chin and cheekbones sharp as a blade, a neat, dark beard, a pair of soulful brown eyes, and a frowning forehead. Those eyes were focused on her. Her gaze went back to the forehead.

Sarah was all too familiar with the lines of this particular frown.

"Ohhhhh, shit," Sarah said, turning back around.

She wasn't sure if she was embarrassed for getting caught ogling this particular man, or annoyed. She went with annoyed. Also, she didn't do embarrassed. Not anymore.

"What is it?" her other friend, Helen, asked.

"I know that guy from high school and middle school and … the cradle, probably. He's one of my brother's best friends."

"Were you teen sweethearts?" Helen asked, waggling her brows.

"Ew. No, we did *not* go out. We were the only two Asian people in my graduating class—different kinds of Asians at that. My parents are from China, and his are from Taiwan. Not that anyone

3

in town cared. They always assumed that we were a breeding pair even when I was actively dating other people."

They had never been very close, but she had appreciated Jake being there. He'd been someone to share a knowing look with across a room or joke with after an exam. But it had turned out that he hadn't deserved any loyalty from her. She sighed. "He's coming this way, isn't he?"

"I'm afraid he's already here."

That last response came in a deep, quiet voice, and Sarah turned herself around once more, slowly this time, caught in his familiar tones. She nodded resignedly in his general direction without looking. "Hey, Jake," she said.

"Sarah."

There was a silence that could have been called uncomfortable, but Sarah was very comfortable with it. She supposed she should attempt to be civil, though, so she broke the silence by taking him in full on and noting grudgingly, "I see you got hot."

She was satisfied when Jake blushed. He stared down at the bottle of beer in his hand and shuffled his feet. It had always been so easy to get to him.

Ugh. *Boys.*

"Thanks," he muttered. Then he added, "And you stayed hot, I see."

"Oh, uh …" She had not expected that. Jake had been a constant presence in her life, but she never thought he'd *looked* at her. Especially after it turned out that he'd been more a friend to her brother, Winston, who was constantly telling her to get lost and treating her like a pesky younger sister, inferior in intellect, strength, and by her very femaleness. Jake had always been there, calm, never contradicting his friend. She knew where his loyalties lay. She sat up straighter. "Yeah, I did stay hot. Thanks."

As an afterthought, she added, "These are my friends, Petra, Helen, and Joanie. We share a practice. Petra's an allergist. Helen's a neurologist. Joanie's our office manager."

A few of Jake's buddies had now slunk closer, looking hopeful. "They're all taken," Sarah added to the group. "I'm not, though."

"Hey, me neither," said Joanie, waving her hand.

It was enough of an introduction for a friendly crowd. Pretty soon, Helen and Petra were rolling their eyes at something a white guy named Josh was saying. Joanie was describing her last acting gig to a rapt audience.

Best of all, with others mingling nearby, Sarah could snag someone else to join the conversation so that she no longer had to chat exclusively with Jake. But, of course, Jake was a lot more polite than she. He always had been. So he stuck with her and exchanged more small talk.

"So how long have you lived in Portland?" he asked.

"Hmm, my residency was four years, I've been practicing for a little under two, so six years."

"And I've been here eight. It's funny we haven't run into each other before."

"Yeah. Funny," Sarah said. "I guess we don't travel in the same circles. I've been delivering babies and starting up my practice, and I guess you—"

"I'm a social worker. I work in the public school system."

"Right. Uh-huh. Social worker. And how's the wife? What was her name again?"

He glanced down at his beer bottle. "Ilse."

"Haven't you heard?" Jake's friend said, crashing into the conversation. "We're celebrating! Liberty! Justice!"

Jake shot him a frown.

"How very American," Sarah said.

Jake introduced his friend, and Sarah promptly forgot his name. "No, really! We're celebrating Jake's freedom," said Greg—or was it Gary?—clapping a hand to Jake's shoulder. "Our friend here just got divorced. But"—he added in a voice that was meant to be discreet— "he's pretty vulnerable now."

Well, well, well. Sarah wondered how the divorce had played with Jake's dad, the very upright Reverend Li.

Jake shrugged. Clearly, he did not want to talk about it. But then, he wasn't the only one who was avoiding touchy subjects tonight. Besides, it wasn't her business. She had her own things to worry about. Or to not worry about.

She was out to celebrate, too. After surgery and a sentinel node biopsy, she'd been declared clear of melanoma. It had been a close call, and she was lucky that the cancer hadn't spread to her lymph nodes.

She had always been careful. She ran and swam and ate healthy food. She used sunscreen. And she was a physician. The diagnosis of Stage II melanoma had come as a complete shock. She still wasn't sure she'd quite processed the fact that … well, she wasn't invincible.

But she was Sarah Soon, ob/gyn, maker of lists, taker of names, kicker of asses, and she had gotten over terrible things before. She always got over them. And she did not give a fuck what Jake Li thought of her.

She turned to another of Jake's almost indistinguishable white guy friends. "So, remind me," she said, "was your name Greg or Gary?"

• • •

A hangover would have been a nice distraction.

But Jake Li woke, as always, feeling gloriously healthy, ready, eager to seize the day—and alone.

The only symptom of last night's indulgence was the fact that his ears were ringing, but that was possibly due to the overwhelming silence of his new, relatively empty rental house.

He grabbed a t-shirt and shorts, grunting and thumping around loudly—and perhaps a little self-consciously—because he had to fill the quiet with something. There was no other person sleeping in his bed. There was no reason to be considerate anymore. And while he was glad that he was no longer married to Ilse, being *not married* was strange.

He went downstairs and made himself a single cup of coffee.

The divorce had been relatively quick and painless, as far as these things went. He and his ex had met in college, in a church fellowship group. They didn't have children. They didn't have a house to sell. They'd been waiting to have children before buying a home. Or maybe it was the other way around. Ilse had been ready to start all of that—they both may have been ready—until she had fallen in love with someone else.

But she told him she believed in her vows. She hadn't acted on her feelings, she said. He was supposed to be grateful for that, but maybe that was worse. The strain and sadness with which she said it: that she wanted to and that she no longer wanted to be with him.

He couldn't even really get angry with her. He was a reasonable mental health professional, and when it came down to it, he had changed. He wasn't the same person who had married her. And when she confessed, he finally admitted to himself that he didn't have those feelings for her anymore.

It still stung, of course. It had been hard lying in bed at night next to her, pretending to sleep as she pretended to sleep, wondering if her sleeplessness was because she was thinking of this other person. She wanted to be a good person. He wanted to be a good person.

He was the one to end it, and after that, everything had been easy.

"Being a good person is such a load of *fucking bullshit*," he said aloud in his empty house.

"Fucking goddamn asshatting bullcrap," he added louder because he could.

And there was no one to say that he couldn't.

And yet, as he came back inside following a short morning run, his thoughts strayed to last night—to his old friend? Acquaintance? His half-realized, half-buried crush? To Sarah Soon, who probably would have been amused at his outburst.

Sarah and her friends had left pretty early, considering. She'd flitted from person to person, making everyone laugh. The one person she hadn't spoken to much was him. And, well, he didn't blame her. He'd been best pals with her older brother, Winston. But Jake was the same age as Sarah, so in the past they'd often ended up together. She was opinionated and not afraid of making fun of Winston—or of him. Winston, in particular, burned with rage when he felt like he wasn't getting his due as the older sibling. Winston had a strong sense of rightness and dignity.

Jake was surprised, though, how disappointed he was that Sarah and he hadn't said much beyond their perfunctory catching up and that she hadn't turned that bright smile on him. The pall of their past—and maybe of Winston's presence—seemed to hang over them, even though it had been at least a decade since they'd seen each other.

The other thing that bothered him about last night was the strain on her face. Despite the laughing and teasing, she looked tired and maybe a little too thin. Had he not known her, he probably wouldn't have been able to tell.

But he knew her. They had a long acquaintance. And although they hadn't talked much through high school, they'd found comfort in each other's presence, maybe because they'd been the only Asian kids in a blindingly white school. Well, there had been some sort of friendship until that last year when she'd been caught with Steve Dixon, who he still hated for reasons he didn't want to think about. Something was up with Sarah now, though. He couldn't mistake the fact that her laugh was forced. She held herself more warily than before—wary was not a word that he associated with Sarah Soon. Maybe not warily, he thought. Stiffly. As if she were injured.

And he had noticed the way her friend Petra watched her like a hawk, half rising in the middle of his conversation with her at one point when Sarah seemed to choke. She'd been faking a cough over something Josh said, it turned out, and the look on Petra's face—the relief—had been palpable.

Jake frowned.

He thought he'd heard all the Sarah news over the years. He'd known she was in Portland and that she was a doctor. He sometimes caught himself scanning crowds for her, wondering if he'd run into her. When his wife—ex-wife—had gone to the hospital for pneumonia, part of him had been waiting and worrying, and a small part of him had been looking out for Sarah Soon. It wasn't that he liked her a lot, but he'd always looked for her when they'd been growing up. It was a habit. He used to find it reassuring to see her black hair tucked behind her ears, the flash of a row of studs and hoops highlighting the delicate curve. When she was in his class at Laketon High—even though they weren't always close—he felt not quite as alone.

And there was the matter of the crush he'd had on her. It was okay to admit it now that high school was in the past. He was still friends with Winston, more out of habit than anything. Jake had stayed in Washington state for college, and Winston had gone to California. Winston was a cosmetic dentist in LA now. And their parents were friends, too. But Sarah never showed up for the holidays, and her rare, brief visits didn't often coincide with Winston's, it seemed. It had been a long time.

Of course, he'd been so preoccupied with the split this year that he could easily imagine he hadn't registered the news that Sarah was possibly sick. Then again, it was pretty obvious that she hadn't kept up with his news; otherwise she would have known that he was getting divorced. And it was clear from the arch of her brow that she hadn't.

But his marriage was officially over, and he felt—clear. It was as if he'd expected the most terrible thing possible to happen but it hadn't been so bad. And even though his friend Greg had gone around telling everyone that he was vulnerable, the truth was that he felt pretty good—no, not just good, he felt really fucking *great*. He felt relieved and lighthearted and free and all of those things that he'd never been allowed to feel for all of his responsible and conscientious life.

Instead of questioning why he was thinking about Sarah Soon a couple of days after his divorce had been finalized, he decided to call Winston. After all, they still talked from time to time, and he hadn't phoned in a while. And he was curious. Concerned, maybe.

"Dude," Win boomed when he picked up. "Whaddup, bro?"

Jake winced. "Hey, uh, dude. Long time."

"You should come down to LA soon and chill. Hook you up with some ladies, amirite?"

It was probably as close as Win was going to get to talking about Jake and Ilse's split, and that was a relief.

They exchanged brief updates about their lives. Winston had moved to a newer, bigger apartment, and he was fighting with the neighbors about their loud dogs. He was talking about a vacation in Belize—and he hinted that he wouldn't be going alone. Eventually, when Winston had exhausted his list of things to report, Jake said, "I ran into your sister last night. Is she—is she okay?"

A pause.

When Winston didn't answer, Jake continued. "It's maybe nothing."

"Are you thinking of making a move on her?"

Jake sighed. "No, man. She looked tired and, I don't know, fragile. She seemed a little off, Win."

Winston sounded reluctant. "I think my mom said she had surgery."

"What kind?"

"I don't know."

"You don't know?"

"Yeah," Winston said.

There was another silence.

"How can you not—and you didn't come see her, did you?" He was aware his voice and his exasperation were rising. "Why haven't you ever come up to see her, Winston? Where are your parents?"

"She didn't want them. She told them she was surrounded by doctor friends and it was really minor."

"And that was convenient for you and them to believe."

"Come on, she didn't say much. It can't have been too serious, I mean. And she *is* a physician. She has that fancy degree. Plus, she was so selfish all her life. Catch me telling my parents they can't come visit."

Then again, Jake couldn't really blame her for telling her parents not to come. Her parents were competent but not at all comforting. He could see why she might prefer the company of friends who obviously cared for her. "She's not selfish. She's the one who was sick. I think she's allowed to decide who takes care of her. But still—"

"Well, she's all right now, isn't she?"

Noting the defensiveness and uncertainty in his old friend's voice, Jake didn't push it. Sarah was probably all right, that was true.

Plus, he'd forgotten about the fierce rivalry between the Soon children. Close in age, Sarah had always been a little better at school, a little better at making friends. Winston got straight As; Sarah got them, too, and was valedictorian. She was an athlete— not the best, maybe, but Jake had admired her lithe body as she tensed on the starting block before each race, her pure, flawlessly clear brown eyes surrounded thickly by short lashes, those dark arched brows. And she had a great sunburst of a smile, which with her beautiful, dark hair had given her lots of admirers. Her last year of school had been tough because of the gossip, but he always remembered her as being vivid and smart. She was no weakling.

Maybe that was why she got away with more than Winston did, or so Winston said.

But she had left home abruptly right after graduation, and she hardly visited her family. And in a lot of ways, her relationship with Winston and her parents seemed suspended right at that moment that she'd gone.

Still. She was the Soons' daughter—Winston's sister—and they hadn't visited her when she was sick. That made him a little angry. "Well, Winston, I know you think she's fine, but I think I'll check in with her again. For old times' sake. My dad would never forgive me if I didn't. Give me her number."

Winston sounded relieved to be getting off so easily. "Always such a do-gooder, Jake. Hang on, let me look for it."

There was some muffled banging, the sound of drawers opening and closing. The rustle of paper.

"You don't have your sister's number on your phone?"

A pause.

"I *got* it. We just don't talk that much. For that matter, she doesn't really talk to my parents that much either. So much for the dutiful daughter they thought they'd have."

"Winston, you're acting like a jackass."

Another pause. "Yeah."

"Hey," Jake said, "you're a grown boy now. You have an amazing apartment and life and all that stuff. Whatever issues you have with your sister are in the past. You'd be torn apart if something happened to her."

He heard Winston take a breath. "You're right. It's in the past. I'm over it."

They exchanged some more *dudes* and *bros*. Had Winston been there, there would undoubtedly have been some backslapping and burping.

"Listen, Jake," Winston said before he hung up. "I know it gets rough and maybe even lonely out there. I've been at it a long time. But you just gotta jump back in, okay? Enjoy yourself, but be careful. Don't get hung up on my sister just because you think you're some sort of white knight. Girls with reputations like my sister's aren't the kinds you should date."

Jake tried to keep the irritation out of his voice. "Don't be sexist, Winston. Sarah didn't do anything wrong. Besides, we've all changed a lot since high school."

"Some more than others. Whatever. We're all good. It's cool."

Jake hung up.

He looked around his empty apartment. He wasn't the same guy he was all those years ago—hell, he wasn't the same guy he was four months ago. And maybe Winston was right about one thing—he should think about jumping back in. But first, he was going to check on Sarah.

CHAPTER TWO

Sarah had vowed not to waste one more minute of her life, and yet, here she was about to give Jake Li an hour of her precious time.

But because she was Sarah Soon, she had a plan: Her phone would go off in one hour and seventeen minutes, she'd frown at it, and then she'd announce that she had to go to the hospital. It wasn't usually her style to fake a call. Painfully honest was her motto in life—sometimes the emphasis was on the pain, but she was almost always honest.

Plus, her new motto was, *Try new things*. She'd had a brush with mortality, and she loved lists. It was a perfect combination of old and new. But that meant she had to now think of things she would normally not do and ... actually do them.

Stupid motto.

So she'd gone water skiing. She'd eaten a funnel cake (okay, half) and ridden on a roller coaster. (The last two items would have worked out better if she hadn't performed them within an hour of each other.) She'd done t'ai chi ch'uan in a park. She'd read *War and Peace*. She was going to try to bike the Big Eastside Trail Loop—as soon as she got more comfortable cycling. She figured getting along with her brother's best friend and leaving with no hard feelings would certainly qualify as a novel experience.

Regret wasn't the word for what he churned up in her—she didn't have anything to regret, after all. But it was hard to leave the past behind, and Jake knew a past her.

Also, there was the possibility that every single thing would end up being reported to her brother, her parents, and maybe even Jake's father. If she refused to hang out with him, they would find that out, too. Not that she cared what they thought.

Maybe it would have been better if she'd just refused.

Then again, Jake hadn't looked like himself. He was harder and ... edgier—and she wasn't just talking about his sharp cheekbones. He was definitely a lot *more* than he'd been as a teenager. He'd always had a great face—eyes that smiled even when he was serious, a contrast with thick, expressive brows. But now that smile had an intensity that hadn't been there before, and it was breathtaking. And then he had all that long, lean muscle over his lanky frame.

She stilled her thoughts. She was not mentally shucking Jake's shirt and pulling down his trousers to contemplate the muscled grooves of his thighs, was she? No.

She shook her head. She had to eat, and she'd gotten to pick her favorite sushi place. At least she could ignore him in favor of her beloved miso soup and a brown rice salmon avocado roll. Her entire hour wouldn't be a waste of any of the precious minutes she had left of life. Hence the timer and the faked medical call. *Carpe diem* after a brush with death and all that.

She wasn't ever in the delivery room anymore. The truth was that she'd cut back on her obstetric practice after her diagnosis. She planned to resume that part of her practice when she came up to full speed again—when she regained that energy she used to have. But she still wasn't feeling it.

No, that wasn't even true. She was feeling too much of everything, and she needed life to slow down a little bit so that she could stop being overwhelmed.

She slid into her booth at the restaurant and closed her eyes.

"Don't tell me I've put you to sleep already," she heard.

She started.

"Geez," she said. "Are you actually a spy?"

"No, just an ordinary, unassuming school social worker."

She blinked. Ugh. It had not been her imagination. He really had grown into his features—no, he looked *good*.

Automatically, she ran her eyes over his button-down, which stretched over boldly sketched shoulders. Ooh, and his sleeves were rolled up, highlighting a masculine stretch of forearm, tendons, and muscles. She couldn't help herself. She peered under the table. Despite the shadow, she noted his long legs in a pair of worn jeans.

"Are you checking me out?"

"Force of habit," she said.

The jig was up, so she tilted her head for a better look. "Bodies are fascinating. I love seeing how everything sort of … hangs together."

She wasn't sure if he was flattered or horrified. She wasn't exactly looking at his face right now. Knowing Jake—and knowing men—probably a little of both. Would it be too forward of her to ask him to give a little kick—nothing fancy—so that she could watch his thigh muscles flex? That would be a treat.

"Runner?" she murmured.

"Erm, yes."

He sounded hoarse, which made her glance up. She shook her head to clear it. She wasn't here to tease him. She didn't plan on flirting anymore—not for a while. And the truth was, she hadn't wanted to for the last half year—not until now. She wasn't even really sure why she was doing this to Jake. *Jake Li*! A boy she'd grown up with! Her brother's best friend! He was practically a sibling. Except he wasn't. And now her scrutiny was making him uncomfortable.

She didn't mind making him uncomfortable.

But maybe he wasn't quite ill at ease, because he seemed to regard her with—oh, that could not be a flare of heat, a little tension in his fine jaw. A clenched hand. A spark from Jake Li.

And from her. She hadn't had felt that thick, warm pulse from down below in a long, long time.

Sure, she was in the clear now. She was alive, and all of her parts were finally functioning smoothly again. When she'd first gotten her diagnosis, she'd been scared and her sexual appetite had fled entirely. And that had been fine. She had other things to worry about. She assumed desire and lust would come back if—*after!* she corrected herself—she recovered. Sex after a significant illness would be joyous and wonderful and all that jazz, she reasoned with herself. It would be great. It would be like reclaiming her life. She looked forward to the time when she anticipated having sex again. But the desire hadn't come back—or at least she hadn't caught any glimpse of the least lick of heat with anyone.

Until she'd seen Jake again. That was truly disturbing to her sixteen-year-old self.

She signaled the waitress, not caring if Jake was ready to order. This wasn't a date. She wasn't dating. She was giving herself a recovery break. And this was an old annoying not-friend catching up. Despite the fact that her whole body tingled with awareness, she was not going to flirt with Jake.

"I'll have the salmon avocado special with the miso soup," Sarah said.

"I'll have the same," Jake said.

The waitress nodded and left, and Sarah regretted ordering so quickly. Now there was nothing between them but a scarred wooden table and an inexplicable tension that seemed to be centered in Sarah's limbs, in her pelvis, in her core.

"So, social worker. What is that? I always figured you'd go and do something more overtly heroic. You know, helping kids in the Outback who've been kidnapped by poachers—"

"Uh, Sarah, isn't that the plot of *The Rescuers Down Under?*"

"Or saving spotty puppies from deranged furriers."

"That's *101 Dalmatians*. I saw both those movies with you and Winston."

She flashed a smile. Okay, maybe she was going to flirt a little.

But Jake narrowed his eyes while obviously trying to suppress his grin. "A fucking Disney movie is what you thought I would do with my life?"

"Jacob Li, did you just say fucking? I'm telling!"

"Who are you going to tell?"

A giggle—a giggle!—escaped her. "Um. God?"

Surprisingly, he laughed, too. "Is that the kind of thing I said when I was a kid?"

They were both still snickering when he leaned back in his chair and the muscles of his chest bunched, stretching his shirt. Yum. No—yuck! This was *Jake*. He was not the person who should be making her gut feel tight. And they were talking about fucking. The word, not the act, but now that was in her head and flooding her body, too.

They shared a long look. He cleared his throat. "Anyway, what's more noble than being a doctor and delivering babies?"

Sarah shrugged. But it was kind of true. She took a calming sip of water. "I am pretty goddamn awesome," she agreed, and oddly enough, instead of rolling his eyes, Jake seemed to smile at her words.

"Tell me about it."

She paused. "It's both the best and worst time for a person. So much pain and so much joy all within minutes and seconds. Plus, it's so messy."

"I'm surprised that you love that it's messy."

"I do. I love that no two birth experiences are ever the same. There's a place for neatness in the rest of my life, and disorder in this part."

She paused, sadness that what she'd just described hadn't been a part of her life recently hitting her unexpectedly. "It's not really just about that work, though. I also love being there for women and girls. I love being the voice of reason—reassuring them about birth control and abortion, answering all the questions I used to have about sex and what's normal. I'm happy to be that informed, assuring presence. That's mostly what I do right now."

And dammit, it was important. She glowered defiantly at Jake, who picked up on her sudden shift in mood. "You're talking like I'd disapprove."

"Winston hates everything his brash, slutty sister does. I'd think you'd have the same opinion."

He seemed ready to answer, but the waitress who came bearing two black and red bowls saved her.

Sarah stared down at the swirls of miso soup. "So, social worker. I can see it. Although, I guess I also thought you'd end up as an astronomer. When you weren't with Winston or rescuing dogs and all that, you were always in your backyard staring through a telescope—maybe wishing to be as far away from Laketon as you could get. Or I thought maybe you'd end up like your dad. Guess I was wrong on all counts."

"I didn't think you'd noticed. But you're changing the subject. I don't disapprove. I'm worried about you. Are you feeling okay? Is your health …?"

She narrowed her eyes at him. "What about my health, Jake?"

It was the way he asked it that almost made her snap. That mixture of concern and some assumed knowledge of her inner workings. Pity, maybe. And it was the fact that she felt a little vulnerable to him—him, of all the people in this damn world. "What did you hear?"

He hesitated. "Winston said you'd had some kind of surgery."

She gripped the edge of the table because the room seemed to spin. "So what, this is a pity date—or whatever? Come here to offer your smug saintly blessings to the poor sick girl?"

She was suddenly so angry. "Guess what? I'm fine. There is no trace of cancer in me."

"Cancer! Sarah—I didn't know."

She found that she was shaking. She did not tremble—even when she'd gotten her diagnosis she hadn't cried once. But now, seeing the concern of someone she'd known for a long time—but who didn't know her—made her irrationally angry. "I fucked that melanoma up. We found it and annihilated it, Jake. I do not need your sad eyes or your worry."

"It's not pity."

"Or admiration of how brave I am. I don't want that. Your sympathy right now is too little too late, Jake."

He sat back, still calm, his face still kind.

"Sarah—"

"Don't try to pretend that you really care about anything that happens to me, Jake. Or that you'll be there for me."

"Sarah, we've known each other forever. Of course I care."

"You haven't always. Remember near the end of senior year, when I got caught with my shirt off at that house party? With that jerk, Steve Dixon? Almost everyone turned on me—my family, my teammates. I went from upright citizen Sarah to foreign temptress in the space of a minute, and I was—and am—neither of those things. Boys catcalled me in the halls. You saw them do it, Jake. You said nothing, but you saw it—and I expected more from you."

Sarah steadied her breath. "You'd known me all your life. And even you—heroic rescuer of children and puppies and all that—even you didn't defend me. I've always thought that maybe you thought I deserved it. Everyone else did."

The last words tumbled out hotly, surprising both of them.

"I *don't* think you deserved it. I never did. I'm sorry." He seemed stricken and sincere.

After a moment, Sarah continued. "The guy's mother freaked out, and suddenly I had a new reputation. It didn't matter that I was born in Laketon, they saw me grow up, I volunteered alongside so many of them. At school, I was nearly stripped of being valedictorian, and your father—your father tried to shame me for bringing bad rep to the Asian community. Most of the other kids in our grade had done similar things, but I wasn't allowed my perfectly normal teen behavior."

Jake shook his head, and Sarah didn't know if he was trying to remember or to deny her words. She didn't care. "That's the problem with being a so-called model minority, isn't it? One measly strike and you're out—even your own people don't want to be tainted by you. But at least your dad wasn't as bad as my parents. I don't think my mother spoke to me again until I got into med school. I left home the day after high school graduation."

"I didn't know that's what happened. I never imagined they'd do something so drastic."

"They weren't like your dad, Jake. He's a minister, but he was a lot more lenient with you than my parents were with Winston and me."

"I'm just putting it all together now. I remember how your parents were," Jake said, slowly. "That's why Winston's such a hard-ass, too."

"Yeah well, it didn't help that I was never the compliant daughter they wanted. For years after that mess, they didn't call me to check up on me—I was the one to keep them informed. It didn't matter that I'd won scholarships. It didn't matter one bit how much I'd done, how hard I'd worked. I had been a good kid. But my parents were effectively gone from my life. I was almost completely isolated and alone, and I was a teenager. That was the worst blow of all."

Jake was quiet. Then he looked right into her eyes. "Sarah, I'm sorry about your parents and that I wasn't a better friend. I should have at least said something to the boys who yelled at you. I—I didn't know how to speak up and I didn't have the whole story, but that's not really an excuse. I should have figured it out."

She *wasn't* upset—it *had* all happened so long ago. But her voice was still unsteady. "Until this point, that was the worst thing to ever happen to me. And I learned from it. I learned that *I* wasn't in the wrong—it was that everyone failed me. And now, a worse thing happened and I survived that, too. I don't want your sympathy, and I don't want your guilt."

Jake's voice was steady and clear. "You're absolutely right."

It was unexpected. It was so strange that he was sitting there taking in her gaze, both determined and sad. She had always thought he would be on Winston's side—that he'd been as horrified and dismayed with her as everyone else in her family. She grouped him with them—in that way, at least. She had been prepared to be defiant. But he wasn't fighting her.

Jake shook his head. "It's funny, but sometimes I have a lot of difficulty reconciling my conservative upbringing with what I see and do now. It's almost like I'm two separate people. I'm one of the few adults at the school who isn't white, and I'm really conscious of that. And you're right, I failed you. I just hope I'm not failing these kids I work with."

She couldn't help herself. "Stop—after Winston left, it's not like we were close. You couldn't have known. It feels like you were a part of it, but I shouldn't expect—I'm blaming you for everything when it wasn't just you. I shouldn't take this out on you."

He put his hand over hers. "I'm still sorry, Sarah."

She didn't know that she was going to accept his apology. Then again, he was the only person who'd ever said to her he was sorry about it. "You were a kid, too."

She pulled her hand away and flopped back in her seat.

They were both silent for a minute, trying to adjust to their new, delicate understanding of each other.

"So, I'm school social worker," he said, changing the subject, and she was grateful for that. "I mean, mostly I just get to poke my nose into people's business, so maybe I haven't changed that much. I try to make sure that the kids can learn—that they have a good environment at school and at home. Sometimes, it's as simple as observing a class or sitting in on parent-teacher conferences. Other times, I'm called in if a teacher suspects abuse, or maybe that a kid is homeless—"

"So you're still totally a Disney rescuer."

"Sarah," Jake growled, "I am not a heartwarming cartoon."

He didn't used to make that kind of sound. He blinked slowly, and she gave a shiver. No. No, Disney didn't make him at all. In an instant, it seemed that he almost shifted before her—from the smiling, nice little Jakey Li she knew to this big, dark glowering creature.

Then it all transformed again under the slyest grin—an expression she was sure he hadn't had before—his eyes making a crinkle at the corners. And he was still dark and big and masculine, but now somehow she wanted to launch herself across the table and see if she could crack that grin wide open.

She kept her ass on her seat. For now.

"I'm just your regular everyday superhero, armed with a smartphone and an intimidating stack of paperwork. Sometimes I feel like I am actually *doing* something. For all we complain about bureaucracy and pushing people around in the system. At least sometimes the heat gets turned on in an apartment. Or a doctor changes a dosage and someone improves—or sometimes I just stop kids from catcalling in the halls."

He held her eyes for a moment.

The waitress brought their plates of sushi. They busied themselves with chopsticks and soy sauce and wasabi. It was a relief and a disappointment to have something else to do. Sarah ate and tried not to study him. But, of course, she couldn't look away.

When he was younger, he always seemed to have a smile—even when he wasn't smiling. When he was a teen, it made him look a little goofy. But now with his sharp cheekbones outlined by the dark beard, his smile was dark and velvety and intense, even as the rest of his long body relaxed in its strength.

She found herself holding a breath as her gaze traveled from the tapered artist's fingers curled around a cup of hot tea and up the decisive slashes of muscled forearm. There was something so compelling about that strong length of limb in front of her.

Dammit.

There were a lot of good reasons she should leave this date— not date—early. But she was starting to get interested in what he had to say, in spite of herself.

The cheery trumpet salute of Johnny Cash's "Ring of Fire" started playing. It was her on call ringtone—a private obstetrics joke.

"Oh," she said, looking at her phone, remembering that she'd set it as a way of escaping from Jake. "I need to take this. In fact, I should probably go. Unless—"

He agreed a little too quickly, it seemed to her. "Duty calls. Who am I to stand in the way of a busy doctor?"

He motioned for the check. Well, that was that.

"Listen," she said, putting some money on the table, "I'm out of line, but from what I heard the other night, it seems as though you have a few things to work through yourself."

He snorted, but she was surprised by her impulse to give something back to him—anything. "We've known each other a long time, Jake, and I know that you try to solve other people's problems. Maybe you should work on your own stuff right now, instead of, say, trying to help your best friend's little sister. Or just do something selfish."

"Live the wild bachelor life? Party with hot ladies?"

His face was neutral, but she could tell Jake was annoyed at her presumption. Well, *good.* "Just, maybe do something that makes you happy—something just for you—really soon."

"What makes you think seeing you doesn't make me happy?"

Again, she didn't know how to answer him. He stood up and kissed her cheek, and she almost couldn't feel his lips on her, because her heart and nerves were jumping.

Almost.

As she headed into the night, she regretted that she'd cut their evening short. It had been fine, after all. And it had cleared the air between them. It was such a rarity to feel satisfied after a conversation with someone who'd known her during those last months of high school—someone who'd known that softer Sarah from long ago.

But that wasn't what she remembered now. That wasn't what was making the skin of her cheek tingle.

She was relieved that she would never have to see him again.

CHAPTER THREE

Greg insisted on showing Jake the dating app before they finished stretching.

"Why do you even have that downloaded on your phone?" Jake asked. "Does Marley know about this?"

"I have it installed to show you," Greg said.

Jake wiped the sweat from his face with the hem of his shirt, accidentally flashing his stomach at two women who sat on a nearby bench. They smirked at him. He gave what he hoped was an apologetic smile, which only made their grins grow wider.

He frowned and glanced down at his shoes.

But Greg seemed oblivious. He was paging through photos of women with increasing speed. "It's a little like a game. If you linger on one photo for more than five seconds, it automatically opens a chat box with the person you're staring at. You can also save people for later, but if you save too many, you get this red filter put over your photo and the only way to get it off is to chat with some of the people you've saved."

"Wow, that sounds high pressure. And sort of judgey."

"It's great. Check this woman out—no, faster."

"How can you even see them?"

"I can see they're hot!"

"You're paging by them so fast I guess it looks like they're aflame."

"I can tell. Besides, I can't pause, because I'm not interested. This is for you."

"Well, can you stop it? Can you exit the app for now?"

Jake gave a sidelong glance to the women on the bench. They were still looking at him with warm appraisal. But now they were whispering. And staring at his chest? Did he have a sign on him that said he was single now, or had he just never noticed women noticing him as much before? No, that wasn't it. In the past, he'd understood that people were eying him, but never before had he felt like he was obligated to act on it—or that Greg might have expected him to strike up a conversation, at least. He supposed he could take it in stride and be flattered—or maybe even ask one of the women out.

Sarah had stared at him, too. He had enjoyed that. He may even have flexed for her.

He shook his head. "Can we go get a juice or something? Maybe we should sit down before I riffle through these women— or does the app only let you do this while you're in motion?"

Greg snorted. "It's not *that* complicated. Let me log out. But I have to make sure I don't—"

Jake began to steer his friend un-gently out of the park.

Later, after they'd settled down with some thick, green drinks, Greg began to complain. "You have to get out there, man."

"Okay, fine. I went out with you guys the other night. We can do that again."

"No, I mean you have to go out and have sex. Just go out and get it over with—maybe do it, like, lots of times."

"Well, I'm not really in a hurry."

"Why not?"

"I just want to find the right—"

"No, no, that's the whole problem. You don't find the right person. You find a convenient person and just do it. And then you find another convenient person, and another, and another and just keep doing it. You do it a lot, and you flush it out of your system."

Jake squinted. "Flush what out of my system? The semen? Does it really work that way? Have you ever done that?"

"Once or twice."

Jake took a deep breath and counted to ten.

Greg said, "Okay, I have never done it, all right? It's more of a theory. That *everyone* believes. You get divorced. You play around. And then maybe you meet someone or maybe not. You want to have sex again, don't you?"

"I'm going to have sex again, Greg. I just want to take my time."

Jake must have looked unconvinced, because Greg launched into another *Hey buddy* speech.

In truth, Jake really did want to have sex—fairly urgently. And if he were very, very truthful, he wanted to have it with Sarah Soon.

But that wasn't quite what Greg meant. Greg apparently had a very specific vision about how Jake needed to act. He wanted Jake to get highlights. He wanted Jake to wear more leather, even though it was summer. And very, very particularly, Greg wanted him to get lots of experience because, admittedly, Jake hadn't dated much before marriage. "Maybe I should cut out the middleman, try to meet women in the dark," Jake suggested.

Greg rolled his eyes and pulled up another dating app for Jake to try.

Sarah Soon, of course, could never be anonymous to him, even with a beekeeper veil and full body armor. He knew the straightness of her spine, the tilt of her head, the snap of her eyes. Her sure voice. Her smooth shoulders. Her fine, firm rear. Very fine.

Still, that wasn't quite what Greg was driving at. Besides, Winston would probably punch him in the face for thinking about his sister that way. No, wrong. Winston would shove Sarah out of the way and put some other girl—any other girl—in front of him. The idea of Winston cartoonishly setting a random woman in Sarah's place made Jake shudder.

"Try to take this seriously," Greg was saying.

"I thought I was supposed to have fun."

"This is because of your upbringing isn't it?"

"Upbringing?"

Greg avoided his eyes. "You know."

"Please elaborate."

"Minister's son. Married your sweetheart and all that."

"Greg, you're accusing me of being one kind of cliché only to get me to act out a different cliché."

"I knew you were going to be offended."

"I'm offended because you're being offensive. I am aware of what everyone thinks I'm supposed to be feeling. Do you think I've been living in the woods? I'm a dude, so I'm supposed to get over it by drinking with my buddies and sleeping with a bunch of women who *know the score* so that I don't end up dancing badly in a track suit like Drake."

"Well, yeah."

"And that's fine for other people if it helps them—no judgment. But I'm me. I want to handle things my way. I have nothing to *get over*. I don't have any steam to let off. We've been apart for months now, and I am okay with my divorce. Pushing me into hookups isn't going to help me cope with things right now. I'd just be going through the motions."

"But the motions feel so good."

"Don't you ever feel trapped by all the stuff you're supposed to do as a man? Maybe it *is* because of my upbringing—or maybe frankly I don't give a shit. Being a man should be about knowing your own damn mind. So here I am saying, *I don't want highlights.* I don't need leather, and I don't want to do what you expect me to do for the sake of doing it."

He was thinking of Sarah when he said it. She had told him to do something for himself. Well, not listening to Greg was sort of like doing something for himself.

But Greg wasn't finished. "Here's the thing that really is killing me: Women are going for you, Jake. That bartender from last night kept eying you and stretching and giving you extra lime wedges—"

"A sign of lust, for sure."

"She never gives *me* wedges. And those women in the park back there were ready to rip your t-shirt to shreds with their teeth."

"They were terrifying."

"That's part of the high! The danger makes it better! Don't you get it? It just seems like such a waste. It's—it's almost unfair."

"Greg, is this about me, or is this about you?"

"What? No, man. Everything's fine. Everything's *fine*."

"It's fine? Then why are you so insistent on making me act like some sort of caricature of a newly divorced man? Like you've got some personal stake in it. Are you talking about what you want or what I want?"

Greg was quiet for a while. Then he gulped the rest of his green drink and set his cup heavily on the table. "It's you. I mean, I don't—I don't actually want those things."

"Then why are you being such a jerk—not even just a plain jerk, but acting like women are pieces that you move around? Why are all the men I'm supposedly friends with being dicks lately?"

Greg couldn't meet his eyes. "You're right."

"You're not usually like this. At least, I hope you aren't."

Greg was still quiet, and instantly, Jake was on alert.

"What's going on, Greg?"

His friend sighed and took a long drink. "Things aren't going great between me and Marley. I just ... I was trying to think of what I'd do if we split up. I thought that you and I could get over our failed relationships together."

Jake blinked. "How do I put this gently? The stuff you've been suggesting doesn't seem to be a good fit for me, or for you."

"Yeah, I guess."

"You've only been together for a few months. I've never seen you react this way before."

"I think I love her but she doesn't feel the same way maybe. I don't know."

"Did you tell her how you wanted more? Did you ask her how she felt?"

"Ye-es? Sort of."

"*Greg.* If you love her, you need to say something to her and show her. You have to do something besides planning for failure."

"You didn't really fight for Ilse."

Jake sat back.

Greg nodded a bit. "Well, that seems significant, doesn't it?"

Male friendship was so weird, Jake thought later, and not for the first time.

After leaving Greg, he went home and took a shower. Ilse had been his friend until they couldn't be friends—or anything—anymore. And maybe that was what he missed most of all about being married. Just the rhythm of it—being able to talk to someone, having a shorthand. He didn't want to have to shuffle awkwardly with stranger. He didn't want to start from the beginning with someone who barely knew him. It wasn't fun or exciting. It was exhausting.

And he had Sarah, who barely could tolerate spending an hour with him.

Who could blame her?

What Sarah said near the end of their last meeting echoed through his mind. *Do something that makes you happy.* Of course, what would've made him happy right then was to kiss her smart mouth. Then again, she was the only person who had actually told him to look at his own feelings in the matter. It was almost like trust: she knew that he had to muddle through on his own. And that was a gift.

He made a decision and picked up his phone. Standing at his kitchen counter, coffee still brewing, he found the address of an animal shelter.

He didn't have to check with anyone. He didn't have to answer to someone else.

He was finally going to do something that would make him happy.

• • •

Sarah's day began with five kinds of sunscreen. A huge dollop for her legs, extra strength for her shoulders and neck. Face sunscreen: she had a less greasy one for her nose and cheeks, a special kind for her eyelids, and another for her lips. She put on a UV-blocking shirt and a hat and stared at herself in the mirror. Of course, she used to do all of this before. Maybe not the special eyelid sunscreen, but she had always been dutiful in cleansing and protecting her skin, eating vegetables, getting exercise. Considering she was an obstetrician, she'd even been good about getting sleep.

But maybe applying all of these lotions to meet her friends for kale chips and wedding planning was a bit of overkill.

"So Petra says she's planning an Indian-Mexican wedding," Helen said when Sarah arrived, "but there won't be any samosas."

"It's a wedding with *nods* to Indian and Mexican tradition," Petra said. "We're just putting in nods to it to acknowledge our respective dads."

Sarah sat gingerly on the oversized couch in the light-filled apartment that Helen shared with her boyfriend, Adam, and took in the assortment of chips, cookies, and vegetables on the coffee table.

"Petra, you're planning this wedding," Helen repeated, "*and there won't be any samosas!*"

It was hard to believe that Helen was getting exercised about hypothetical food when there were so many real snacks arrayed in front of them right now.

Then again, that was Helen. "What is even the point of your being half-Indian? *Caught between two cultures, not sure where to turn*, and you don't even get the damn food. You can bet that if Adam and I get married, there will be a giant dim sum steamer tower in lieu of or in addition to a huge, huge wedding cake. With sprinkles. I can have sprinkles on my wedding cake, right?"

Petra sighed and turned to her less carb-obsessed friend. "Sarah, how are you feeling?"

"I'm picturing feats of dim sum architecture."

"If I don't get samosas, then she doesn't get kale anything," Helen said from deep within the couch cushions.

Sarah took a deep drink of tea and tried to concentrate on the task at hand. This was usually her part in their friendship and in the Pearl District practice all three of them shared: keeping things on track, making sure Ts were good and crossed and the dots were adequately dotty. She was so used to being the one who kept things running that she should have been alarmed to find herself letting go of these tasks—letting go of that role.

But she was tired. And she was thinking about Jake Li two days later. She was still half angry about the fact that he'd met with her to check up on her. But why? Her pride was piqued? Because he hadn't called again? Because he was the one who had managed to rouse her latent libido? Stupid Jake, always making her care about what he thought of her.

She shook her head, trying to clear her mind. "Look, Ian runs two restaurants. He knows food better than any of us."

"And hospitality," Petra said. "That's why he's in charge of food, coordinating, and pretty much everything else. It turns out that

Ian has a lot of opinions about his wedding. Plus, it'll be fairly small. No bridesmaids, no maid of honor, no best man."

Petra pulled out a file and flicked it toward Sarah. "I thought you'd enjoy this. It's color coded."

Helen's eyes widened as she leaned over to take in Ian's plans. "Ian's almost as organized as Sarah."

Sarah flipped through the work and admired it dutifully. "I think I love him. What's more, I think I understand him better than you ever will."

"He's making me look bad," Petra admitted cheerfully.

"So why are we here?"

"I do need to figure out something to wear—"

"Don't do the dress on the cheap," Helen warned, remembering Petra's predilection for bargain bins.

"I promise I'll make you look at so many dresses that you'll dream in tulle. But there's still time to think about it. Anyway, Sarah's been sick. I've been busy. The other thing I thought we could talk about was a bachelorette party."

"Are you allowed to plan your own bachelorette party?" This was Helen. "I hate bachelorette parties."

"Well, we can do what we want with this one. It doesn't even have to be a bachelorette. It can be a shower. Or a girls' weekend. Or a space witch coven bonfire-slash-marshmallow roast."

"No 3D movies and no road tripping," Sarah said.

"Of course not," Petra said solicitously.

"You know, Petra, for a doctor, you sure have a lousy bedside manner. Stop treating me like I'm going to expire on this gigantic sofa. I take it back. Let's drive across the whole damn state. We can stuff ourselves into a car and hit every hippie farm stand you want. I don't need to be near life support at every moment. I am not dying."

"Well, maybe I don't want to go on a road trip with your grumpy ass."

"That is not the point. You've been pussyfooting around me since my diagnosis. It's creeping me out."

"But you aren't yourself, Sarah. I thought I'd have to hold you off from plunging straight back into work, but you're only coming in a few times a week. You've been spacey. You disappear for long periods of time and come back with bracelets from Six Flags. That worries me."

"I don't feel ready to get back to full time. I need to do this slowly."

"But you love work. And you wouldn't cut down unless—"

"I do love work. I'm just not … in the right head space."

Helen popped up. "In the right head space?" She felt Sarah's forehead theatrically. "No fever. You must really be dying then, because I've never heard this much woo woo come out of your mouth."

Sarah laughed, but she also felt like crying. Sometimes, she and Helen butted heads, but right at this moment, she needed her friend's ribbing.

They did end up looking for dresses—online. For maybe three minutes. Then Petra got distracted by a text from her mother and ended up talking her down from a boyfriend crisis. Helen started playing a game on her phone. Ordinarily, Sarah would have been in there, putting together a Pinterest board. And she did pull together four dresses in styles that Petra would like and three pairs of sparkly shoes, and checked Petra's online calendar, and set up an appointment at a bridal shop near their office. But then she simply sent the date and links to Petra and didn't harass her friend about it. She didn't feel like marshaling her friends to action today. By the time Sarah was ready to leave, it seemed like they'd planned nothing. And now that she had a block of free time, she slathered on more sunscreen, pulled on her hat, and took herself to the park.

It was her favorite walk of late, but as she crossed under a line of trees, she saw, as if conjured from her thoughts, a familiar figure ambling up to her.

Except he had a dog—an excited, floppy-eared, russet mutt who seemed happy to see her—and to see trees, and grass, and ants, and leaves, and rocks.

It was a little too much for both Sarah and the dog to take in. "I didn't know you lived in this neighborhood," Sarah said, crossing her arms as Jake Li approached.

He flashed that crinkly-eyed grin at her, and she found herself holding her breath. "I'm not far—just in Laurelhurst," he said. "But I've been doing a thing lately where I go to different parks in Portland. It sounds a little weird, right?"

"No, that sounds …" She'd thought about doing something similar—she *was* doing something similar.

She didn't finish the sentence. Instead, she bent down to the dog who immediately started sniffing and licking her fingers enthusiastically. Her special sunscreen blend was apparently delicious.

"Her name is Mulder. Fox Mulder."

"You didn't name her Scully?"

"Well, she's easily spooked, and I found her standing on top of the kitchen counter this morning. So I thought it would be more appropriate."

Tail wagging happily, Mulder was now investigating some unusual activity near the base of an oak.

Sarah didn't know why she suddenly felt exposed and vulnerable. Jake wasn't even looking at her. He was keeping his eye on the dog. But she wanted to pull her hat down and button the top button of her special UV protection shirt.

"You didn't mention that you had a dog."

"I got her from a shelter yesterday, so we're still getting to know each other."

He sent a fond smile the dog's way. They weren't getting to know each other. He was already head over heels in love.

It was cute, but noticing his attractiveness sent a zing of fear through her spine. *Not again*, she said to herself. *Oh god, not again.*

CHAPTER FOUR

Jake was surprised at how happy he was to see her. Mulder certainly was delighted too, given the way she'd almost pulled the leash out of his hands as they went to meet Sarah.

Sarah seemed reserved, which was unlike her. Although it was probably the hat and the oversized shirt contributing to the sense of distance. She'd never been big to begin with, but she seemed almost to shrink inside this clothing.

He found himself very much wanting to see her arms and shoulders bared, like they had been the first night he'd reconnected with her, her sharp elbows and delicate wrists.

"I didn't take you for an *X-Files* fan," Sarah said.

He could surprise her. That was a nice feeling. It had been a long time since he'd surprised anyone.

"I like Scully," he said.

"Of course you do."

"No, I mean, I like Gillian Anderson, but I also like how the character thinks. I like her skepticism that hides this deep well of feeling and belief."

A deep well of feeling and belief? Ohh-kay. "So you're Scully and your dog is Mulder. Except she's more of a *trust everyone* sort."

"I'm not saying I'm like Scully."

"Maybe you are."

There was a pause.

"I'm surprised you were allowed to watch *The X-Files*."

"I think you have set ideas of how my dad was."

"My parents were strict about some things," Sarah said. "A lot of parents in Laketon were. Some were worse than mine, even."

He suddenly remembered that now. Winston always came over to Jake's house to watch TV, even when the Soons were still pulling long hours at their hardware store. Jake's father was the preacher, but in a way, his dad was looser, more inclined to forgive skipped classes and broken curfews. He was certainly easier than Sarah's parents or his next-door neighbors, the Kheels. Jake's father was perhaps more focused on inward behavior. Fun times.

He was about to say something more when a tall, tan woman barreled between them.

"It's *you*—you're real," she said.

Jake did not know how to respond to that.

"I saw your picture on SnogAppeal, that dating app. I saved you on my wish list."

Sarah stepped out from behind the woman. "You're on SnogAppeal?"

"Uh, yeah."

"Wow, my friends and I thought you were just some model they used to attract customers. Like, look at how diverse it is while still having hot dudes. Unless—you are really on the site, aren't you?" The woman peered at him suspiciously.

"No, I'm …" He glanced up at Sarah quickly. "I'm really on the site."

The woman followed his gaze to Sarah. "And this isn't your girlfriend or wife?"

"No, of course not," Sarah replied for him, a trifle too quickly, he thought.

The woman—she introduced herself as Ashton—went to pet Jake's dog and moved a little closer.

She was saying something, and Jake was trying not to be rude, but he could see Sarah was not going to stay. He was sneaking glances at Sarah while he absent-mindedly answered a few questions about Mulder. Sarah looked unhappy. With him? And he was torn about it, because he did feel guilty, almost as if he were betraying her. But he ought to get himself out there, at least for his mental health, right? Except he was regretting joining SnogAppeal right now. Above all, he really didn't want to talk to Ashton at this moment, even though she was being nice to his dog. She was driving Sarah away.

Jake began to tug on the leash, but Mulder was rolling around and enjoying the attention a little too much and Sarah had already waved perfunctorily and started to walk away, so finally, he picked up his dog—his heavy, squirmy dog—and went after her.

"I'll see you on the Internet, maybe?" the woman called.

"Why'd you leave?" Sarah asked, whirling on him as soon as they got out of earshot. "You should've at least gotten her phone number."

"How do you know I didn't?"

Sarah stopped and looked skyward. She rubbed her arms as if she were cold. "She was one minute away from asking you out."

"I don't want to go out with her."

"Why not? She's got great legs and she liked your dog—and your dog loved her."

"My dog seems to love almost everyone and everything. Trees, people, grass, sky, sunshine, refrigerators, dead leaves, empty bottles—"

"Tall, tanned brunettes who seem relatively okay."

"I am not my dog."

They stared at Mulder, who was delightedly sniffing a trash bin. "No, you're not."

A beat.

"I should go home," she said.

"I'll walk you."

"It's broad daylight and not far."

"I want to."

She said nothing to that but led him and a bouncy Mulder around another path, past the high school, then down a few leafy, quiet streets. Sarah asked him a few questions about the pet shelter and kept up a steady patter about Portland parks and neighborhoods. When they turned up to the small, well-kept house, she paused and said, almost reluctantly, "Well, this is me."

She still hadn't looked at him, and her enormous hat shrouded her face. He couldn't read her expression. "Let's go through the gate," he suggested, his voice a little creaky.

It suddenly seemed important for her to let him into her space. Whatever Sarah once felt about him seemed to be changing, and half-formed instinct told him to seize this opportunity—but only if she was willing. He could have stepped over the gate without her answer. Hell, he could have just left her there, mysterious and untouchable under her layers. But he had always liked her from afar, and now she was here and within his reach, and he was not the awkward kid he had been. He was a person who could be with her. So he stood patiently, his stomach twisting and plunging as he waited for a response from underneath the brim of her damn hat. It was an effort not to lean his body toward hers, as he wanted to, to offer her shade, to test her warmth. Under the sun, he felt a bead of sweat on his forehead, and he suddenly wished that he'd thought to protect himself from exposure, too.

And then she looked up at him, her eyes running over him so thoroughly and swiftly that he almost felt fingertips brushing his cheeks and shoulders. She gave a sharp nod, at odds with the soft confusion of her face. She opened the gate, and Mulder tumbled inside ahead of both of them and started rolling in a patch of clover.

He let out a long breath and stepped inside, still nervous for some reason, trying to take everything in.

"I bought it a couple of years ago," she said hurriedly.

He took another step and sniffed the air. "Mint," he said.

"Yeah, pots and pots of it." She waved at a row of hodgepodge containers. "I should probably try and tend it or something. But it seems to do fine without me."

She went further along, heading toward the shadow of her porch, and he followed, taking in the yard in long sweeps. It was a little less neat than he'd expected it to be. A pile of stones sat in a corner, as if she'd planned on setting them on the path but had forgotten them. A small patch of pansies was to the side, near a low, fat bush.

It was a mistake, he thought, to loop Mulder's leash on the porch railing, because now his hands didn't have anything to hold. Sarah had finally taken off her hat, and she stood on the porch, her eyes gleaming as she seemed to study him.

He took a step up and she didn't object. He would have bound up the rest of the way in victory, but she stopped him. "You know, there's probably still time to catch up with Ashton. She looked like she was just getting ready to do a few circuits of the park."

He paused, temporarily confused that she'd stopped his forward momentum. "Wait, who's Ashton?"

"You know who she is," she said impatiently. "The woman who recognized you from the dating app. The one with the legs."

"You're going to have to be more specific than that."

She groaned and thwacked him gently. The shock of contact— her hand, his shoulder— crackled up through his body and fizzed like a thousand bubbles. Sarah brought him alive. She always had.

"You're jealous," he said, delighted.

A pause. "You don't have to look so happy about it."

She turned away, but with nimble fingers, he pulled off her hat, and she couldn't hide her expressive face anymore.

"Have you ever thought about it? About us?" he asked.

"I—" She frowned fiercely. "I never let myself."

"Why not?"

"You were my brother's best friend, and I was trying to be cool and rebellious and you were—"

"A dork?"

That stung. But it had been true.

"No, that wasn't it."

"You don't have to lie, Sarah. I was quiet, skinny, and spent a lot of time staring through telescopes."

"I don't lie, especially not when it counts. You were not some ridiculous stereotyped shorthand. You were your own person, and I admired that. Maybe some stupid kids didn't understand how much you were yourself. You always stood up for people and for your beliefs."

"Mostly," he reminded her. "And it's not like you didn't do that, too."

"Mostly," she said echoing his words—and oddly, his guilt. But she continued, "I took great comfort in having you around, in knowing you even though we weren't best buddies. I remember teen dramatics and sometimes feeling alone, but then I'd see you there, observing—observing me, like you were really taking me in—and I'd think *There's someone who will always know me*, no matter how close or far apart we were. So, I didn't think about us, but I guess I did."

"What about now?" He took another step, and she came forward to him. Her eyes were level with his, her face, her lips. He wasn't sure who leaned forward first, but quietly and suddenly, her warm breath mingled with his. Her soft, round cheek brushed his. Her mouth pressed firmly against his, and he slipped his fingers into her dark, warm hair and pressed her even closer.

He licked into her as she opened, and the trickle of arousal that had been there emerged in a full gush, filling his body, his abdomen, his groin. He felt it down to his heels. He pressed his hands down her body, down those small shoulder blades like butterfly wings, down her lithe back, down to the firmness of her ass, and he pulled her into him, closer and closer.

Her mouth opened still wider into him, and her moan rose up through her throat and into his. Her breasts rubbed into him before she pulled away slightly and then slammed the full force of her rounded body against him once more and just … just dragged her perfect, small breasts and thighs and arms across him, causing all of his nerves to shrill and buzz and making him dig his fingers deeper into her bottom, bringing them down lower, under the curve of her cheeks, and lifting her against his hardness.

It was his turn to moan as her sure hand slid under his t-shirt, her fingers splaying just under his belt. If they pulled each other any closer, they wouldn't be able to breathe, not that either of them was doing too well on that front. Her panting filled his ear, and he felt another painful pulse of arousal along his cock as she dragged the vee of her thighs along it once more.

"Dammit, Sarah," he whispered.

And that was what made her release him abruptly. She pulled away, swayed back into the shadow, still breathing heavily, as he gritted his teeth and willed his body to gentle and relax, as he forced himself to let her retreat. He dragged his fingers off her butt, a caress that came around nearly to her front, and let his hands drop slowly.

She stared at his hands, too.

When she finally spoke, her tone was firm. "We can't do this. There's too much between us already. Too much knowledge."

She said it as if it was final, but her tousled hair, her flushed face and darting eyes were anything but decided.

"I don't even know what that means."

"It means I know you well enough—I know me well enough—that even though there's attraction that it's a bad idea."

When he didn't say anything, she went on. "We're both … vulnerable right now."

The way she said that word, vulnerable, with a grumble in her voice as if it irritated her to apply the word to herself, made him almost laugh, even as his heart did a painful flip-flop.

"Why isn't this the time, then?" he asked. "This is the perfect time. Because nothing of significance ever happens if we aren't even a little vulnerable."

"The last thing I want is significant," she said, waving her hand a little.

But it was a false gesture. Because of that tremor.

He took a step up closer to her but not touching.

"I dare you to tell me again that you think that was nothing, that you didn't feel very much. Maybe you're right, there's too much between us. There's already too much between us—we are very acquainted with each other. But everything I know about you makes me want you more, makes me want to learn more. I know you, and I know enough to tell you that you were almost angry and you wanted more. I dare you to deny that you're warm and pliant and ready to fuck me right now, right on these hard stone steps."

Her breaths were shallow again and mouth open. Her eyes moved over him as if she couldn't believe the things coming out of his mouth. He could barely believe them himself.

She shook her head. "I don't know what to feel."

"Well, let me know when you figure it out."

He swallowed back his disappointment, but as he calmed his breathing and unwound Mulder's leash from the steps, a small glimmer of hope shone steadily in the distance. She hadn't said no. She had responded to him fiercely. She wanted him, and that was more than he had ever expected.

He didn't look at her, because even one look would undo him. As he turned to walk down the steps, his dog came to him and trotted around him, only the wild whipping of her tail betraying any of her feelings. He started down the path, through the gate. But he knew Sarah's eyes were still on him, still searching for him, as he disappeared from her view.

CHAPTER FIVE

Who would've thought Jake Li had it in him.

It wasn't just the kissing, the hot press of his chest against hers, his lips, the tickle of his beard, the hot wash of his tongue. It wasn't just how unexpected and forceful the grooved muscles of his arms had been.

It wasn't just the large and intriguing erection, although that was a big part of it. *Who would've thought Jake Li had it in him, indeed?* But his words, his voice. His eyes like a hand all over—

Sarah shut the door firmly behind her, gave it an extra shove, smoothed out her shirt, and tried to put herself to rights. But her body was still sunk deep with lust, and even her own touches sent echoes of feeling through her.

She was in so much trouble.

She ripped off the hat and the shirt and sank down to the hallway floor.

She'd stared after him for a long time as he'd left with his dog, part of her mind occupied with his promise to take her on her stoop, part of her admiring his ass, and a very small part of her wondering how he could walk with such a huge and very admirable hard-on.

Slowly, it turned out.

Now, with uncomfortable wood floor underneath her, she could almost imagine it might be like reclining on the steps with Jake's head between her legs. She held that image in her mind, moved her fingers, and there it was—more of an ... anticlimax for how little it did for her. Her vagina gave her a couple of grudging ripples, and she let out a long-held breath. She sighed, got up, zipped, and went to wash her hands.

At least any whisper of doubt that her body was interested in having sex again no longer lingered. Too bad it only seemed interested in sex with Jake.

But she didn't call him the next day. She didn't call him after she woke up the next morning and went into the office. She didn't call him in between patients, when she totted up just how many birth control pills she'd prescribed. She didn't call him before she took a one-off hip-hop dance class filled with earnest white women and then crossed that off her list forever.

But she thought about him before she pulled cool sheets over herself at night, and when she should have been considering how expensive her malpractice insurance was versus how many—how few—procedures she was taking on nowadays.

The ball was in her court, but her court was no place for balls of any kind, especially not—ugh, she was not going to start making dumb jokes about Jake's balls now, was she?

It was too difficult for her right now, and she wasn't going to beat herself up for being a coward when she wasn't one. Because despite what he'd told her, her whole being was too soft right now. Especially around him. Especially around a person who reminded her of the things she'd had to do when she was still so young and so vulnerable. The things she'd done to make herself into Sarah Soon, ob/gyn, maker of lists, taker of names, kicker of asses.

• • •

The third time Jake ran into Sarah accidentally was at a chichi bar in the Pearl that Sarah said was owned by one of her friends. Said friend—Ian—was laughing with a big, blond man, Adam. Sarah introduced the two to Jake grudgingly. Of course, they noticed right away how Jake gazed at Sarah and how Sarah avoided looking at Jake. Their suspicions were immediately raised. Neither seemed cowed by Sarah's glare.

"I am not going out with Jake, and don't you dare say a word to Petra about it if you value your life," she'd told Ian.

"Sarah's too ethical to really harm him," Adam told Jake cheerily.

"And if you try something sneaky, I'll use my last dying breath to let Petra know that you violated the spirit of the Hippocratic oath if not the letter," Ian added.

She swore at them, but to Jake she barely grunted a goodbye.

He'd made Sarah Soon run from him.

The fourth time they met by chance was at the sushi place.

She didn't actually say that this was her stomping grounds, but her face was fairly transparent. He'd had fewer squabbles over territory and friends with his ex-wife. In fact, he hadn't had any at all.

"What? The food is good!" he said, a little defensively.

Sarah scowled, but not before he saw reluctant agreement flitting over her face.

"Let's make that order to go, please," she said to the waiter.

And he almost felt a little guilty, because while the food had indeed been good, another part of him had showed up on purpose in hopes that he'd run into her here. But he definitely did feel guilty because he was there waiting for his date to show up.

It was a jerk move. But Sarah hadn't called him, and he wasn't going to go to her if she wasn't ready. And, of course, by now he'd had time to become unsure of himself.

He was no longer married, after all. He had thought he was going to be with Ilse for the rest of his life. Everyone expected him to do certain things: be sad, cover it up with empty socializing, not have feelings for a while. He'd tried to resist that, but aside from his dog, who'd love him even if he didn't give her liver treats, he wasn't getting much support. So he was going on one date with a woman who over chat seemed smart and sensible and, above all, cautious. And he was going to enjoy himself. Cautiously.

At this sushi restaurant that Sarah frequented.

Then again, his excuse was that he didn't really know a lot of places, and this one was pretty much perfect: quiet, with genuinely good food, and a little too antiseptic to be romantic. He was bringing a great attitude to this first date.

Sarah took a seat near him but not at his table.

"Why is it that I've accidentally run into you more in the last month than in the last six years we've both lived in the same city?"

"I didn't go out that much when I was married."

Sarah grunted, but she seemed to relax a bit.

"We lived a little farther out," he continued. "I cooked more. And now I'm in a new neighborhood, and I'm trying to see the city."

She nodded. "You cook."

"I try." She leveled a look at him, and he held up his hands. "I did most of the food prep growing up."

"I didn't know that."

"Well, I figured out how to not turn a piece of salmon into a dry, cottony slab, to salt the pasta water, to chop everything for a stir fry the same size. I can turn out a decent meal."

Before she had an opportunity to ask why he was then *here*, his SnogAppeal date, Lydia, came hesitantly to his table.

"I'm sorry to interrupt," she said glancing from Sarah to Jake.

He stood up abruptly, almost knocking his water glass over.

"Lydia. Hi. I'm sorry; I was just talking to my … friend. This is Sarah."

"Are you sure you aren't—"

Sarah said quickly, too quickly for his liking, "It's cool. We're not—"

And he said, "It's—we're just—"

Lydia still hadn't sat down.

"My food is going to be here really soon, and I'll be leaving," Sarah said.

She nodded as if for emphasis, and something about seeing her pointy little chin go up and down decisively annoyed him. She didn't have to pretend she didn't like him when clearly she did. But now that the clock had officially started running on his date with another woman, it was probably not the time to get into that particular argument.

He turned to Lydia. She had soft brown hair in an old-fashioned pageboy and a pair of cat eyeglasses. He had swiped her because she seemed dreamy and gentle in her picture. But maybe that was just the filter, because in person, Lydia seemed pretty sharp—if shy. Her left eyebrow was raised, and she still seemed to be focused on Sarah. Well, so was he.

The waiter came by with a menu for her, and Lydia stayed perched at the edge of her chair. Like Sarah, she looked poised to flee. Great, now he was driving women away in pairs. Maybe it would become exponential as time passed.

"We were just talking about how Jake recently moved to a new neighborhood and is feeling up to exploring the city again."

"Oh, are you new to Portland?" Lydia asked.

He darted Sarah a look. "No, but I used to live in University Park."

"With your ex-wife?" Lydia gestured at Sarah.

"I am not his ex-wife."

"Did you know the ex?"

"No, never met her—"

"Maybe we should stop talking about Ilse," Jake interjected.

They studied their menus in silence.

"The salmon roll special is really good," he said to break the silence.

"Ilse. I picture someone tall and blond. You must have made a striking couple."

"Not anymore," Jake said, gritting his teeth in a smile. "So Lydia, you're a project manager?"

"For a planning firm. I get a lot done."

"Erm, what kinds of projects do you manage?"

Lydia ignored the question. "So how do you two know each other?"

"We grew up in the same town."

There was a silence.

A waiter came and asked for their orders. "I'm going to try that salmon roll special," Lydia said. "Separate checks. And I'll take it to go."

That was quick.

"Are you kidding me?" Sarah muttered.

Lydia shook her head. "I don't know what's going on here, but I've been on enough of these things to be suspicious. And I think that's perfectly justified. You two know each other, and you obviously have some kind of history. My doubts are probably going to cloud the entire evening, even after you leave. Jake's already uncomfortable."

She turned and addressed herself to him gently, "Jake, your forearms are A-plus. As fantasy fodder, you seem amazing. But you're not just hot—you're complicated, and while that might have been appealing when I was in my twenties, I'm not up for that now. Even if I don't know you, I know myself. And I can already tell this isn't going to work, so I'm going to cut my losses and go home and watch Netflix and eat some good—according to you—sushi."

The waiter looked left and right, unsure what to do. Jake couldn't really help him.

"Well. I kind of respect that," Sarah said grudgingly. "And the sushi *is* good."

"Like I said, I get a lot done."

"I'll have the salmon roll special to go, too," said Jake. "But I insist on paying for both."

Jake pulled out his wallet, but Lydia was already going to the counter with her credit card out. In a moment, she took out her phone and leaned against the wall.

"This is not awkward at all," Jake said.

"I'm never going to be able to come here again, and it's your damn fault for bringing a date to my sushi place. They think I'm the third in a love triangle. I'm supposed to be the cool-but-mysterious regular."

"Well, now you're the cool-but-mysterious regular with an active love life."

"I have no love life."

"Two days ago on your porch you did."

Both swung their heads guiltily toward Lydia, who was leaving with her takeout order. She gave a little wave.

"In another time, she and I could have been friends," Sarah said.

"Yeah, I wish we'd met under better circumstances, too."

"Oh. Well, I'm sorry my presence at *my* restaurant ruined it for you then."

"I don't like her that way. But she was right. It wasn't ever going to work out. She was direct about it. She wasn't being malicious. She reminds me of you."

Sarah was quiet for a moment, then nodded. "Sensible girl."

"Like I said, I liked her."

The waiter dropped two bags of food in front of them.

Sarah got to her feet. "I should get back."

"We could eat together."

When she said nothing, he continued. "We should at least talk."

"Our talking is what drove Lydia away."

"And now the only one left in the room is the giant elephant."
Again, she said nothing.

"Come on," he said. "Bring the takeout to my house."

He left enough cash for both their dinners, slung the bags over one wrist, and put his hand on the small of her back to steer her out. She came willingly.

"I hope elephants like sushi," he heard her mutter.

CHAPTER SIX

The dog bounded up to both of them when they got inside, lavishing Sarah and Jake with the kind of exuberant affection and enthusiasm that they were not displaying toward each other.

He took her jacket from her and held out his hand for her purse, too, giving it a tug as he slung it on a peg as if to make sure she wouldn't make a quick escape. She followed him to the kitchen while he put out more food and water for Mulder, then out to the backyard where Mulder ran after them snuffling happily. Sarah noticed that at one corner, Jake had set up a telescope.

Jake put their plastic bags on a rusty patio table. He produced a cushion for her chair and stepped back inside to get a couple of water bottles.

They ate mostly in silence. At first, Sarah needed to get her jangling thoughts under control. But the evening was calm and quiet and she didn't want to fret anymore—so she stopped worrying about what she was supposed to do next. She watched him, the beetling of his brows as he swiped his sushi through soy sauce and wasabi, the wash of calm on his face when he glanced over at Mulder, the inquisitive but veiled expression whenever his gaze moved over to her.

She may have shivered a bit, and he noticed that right away, too. Because he pulled a blanket out of a bench seat, shook it out, and wrapped it around her, pausing to drape it around her neck and take in a quick breath of her, and then retreated back to his seat.

She'd forgotten how patient he was. He would probably go slow.

The licking fire in her gut spread.

She put down her chopsticks and hitched the blanket higher around her. He wasn't eating. She wasn't eating. She picked up the containers and began to wrap everything up methodically. He took everything from her hands and followed her into the house. Mulder wasn't nearly so polite. She bolted through the door and skidded across the tile, her claws clacking merrily, and she ran off to another room, leaving them alone.

He put the containers—hers and his—in the fridge.

No easy escape—at all.

Then again, she didn't really want to run. She was here because she'd made a decision at the restaurant. She had gotten in his car. She had come to his house. So she took a deep, steadying breath and pulled in the faint rain-damp smell of him, and she felt her chest warm in anticipation.

"All right," he said, putting himself across the kitchen from her. "Let's talk."

He squared his shoulders and directed his liquid gaze toward her.

"I do want you," she said. She could hardly breathe, but she had to get the next words out. He took a step forward. She held up her hand. "But I'm scared. And nothing will make me angrier than you dismissing my fear or daring me—daring me!"

"What?"

"Your words: *I dare you to tell me again that you think that was nothing. I dare you to deny that you're*—I don't know, ready to fuck me on the steps! I can't remember exactly." She clenched her fists. "Does that reverse psychology really work? I'm not a child on the monkey bars. You don't get me to do things by saying, *I dare you.*

54

I'm not a coward for being cautious. You let me down once. And yes, I know we were both kids at the time, but that sharpens my fear, Jake. I felt everything more back then, and that makes it difficult to get past it. This can't ever be some simple one-night stand—this can't be, because there's already too much between us."

"I know, and that's not what I'm after. Like you said, we know each other too well. But also not enough, Sarah. I have always liked you and wanted more."

Another step closer.

She said desperately, "I don't want you to tell me that the past doesn't matter. Because it does. We've hurt each other before. I—I threw a rock at you once. I called you terrible names."

"You were five."

"It wasn't just that time. Think of how much more damage we could do now."

"I'm sorry for how your parents and Winston treated you. I'm sorry about the other kids and parents in town, that my dad shamed you in front of a whole congregation. I should never have stood by and just watched. And I regret that I didn't say anything to you back then, because I did and do care about you. I'm asking for a chance."

She nodded.

Another step.

He was close.

She closed her eyes.

"Tell me what you want me to say," he said.

"I want you to say that me kissing you will be all right."

"I can't tell you that. But I will try to make it good."

• • •

Once again, he took her hand. He led her down the hall to his bedroom, and he shut the door.

"I feel like you're trying to make sure I don't run away," she said.

"I just don't want the dog barging in, but sure."

She laughed nervously.

"Come on," he said, tugging her to the bed.

The bedroom was dim. There was a bureau with a few coins on it, a nightstand, a charger, and a wide, slightly rumpled bed. He led her there. They took off their shoes and sat cross-legged on the covers, facing each other.

"I feel like we're in some sort of new-age therapy session. *Hi, I'm Sarah. I like cruciferous vegetables and list-making. Lately, I've felt adrift.*"

"Okay," he said, putting his hand on her knee. He began to stroke his way up her thigh. "*I'm Jake. I like a woman who speaks her mind. I like playing catch with my dog. And I'm a little nervous right now.*"

"Why are *you* nervous?"

"Well, here you are, despite yourself. I've brought you here with promises ..." His voice dropped low, and she felt a little throb right between her legs. "And now you're here and I want to pull all your clothing off and stare at you and lick you everywhere and fuck you. But it probably won't be that good for you if I try that all at once. So you're going to have to tell me what we should do first."

They looked at each other, a little surprised at what had come out of his mouth. "I'm never going to get used to hearing you swear, Jake."

That sly grin again. *Well.*

She nodded. "Take off your shirt."

He trailed his fingers down her thigh and reached down to his waist. He pulled up the hem of his shirt, and Sarah stared at the shadowed spot where his skin began, watched as he pulled his clothing up slowly, over his head, and dropped it on the floor beside her.

He was lean and strong, his muscles forming long cuts along his shoulders, his chest. The deeper grooves of the forearms she so admired tightened as she rose to her knees to touch his faintly gleaming skin. Just a touch. Two fingers in a hot slide over his pectoral muscle, a palm skating down his abdomen.

She could hear his breathing. Or was it hers?

"Sarah."

"Take off your jeans and lie down."

His gaze at her was almost angry as he unfolded himself and stood beside her. She turned her head and stared at his zipper, at the strained lines tracing his erection. She watched the pop of each metal tooth as he undid his pants and pulled everything down in one movement.

She could see all of him now. His head bent, his torso tense, that thick, hard cock, and the severe lines of his legs, poised to spring.

"*Down.*"

He lowered himself gingerly, and she watched intently as one leg came up beside her, then another.

As if he couldn't help himself, he brought his hand to his cock and took a long pull.

She threw off her t-shirt at that and pulled her own jeans down.

It wasn't until he rose to look at her that she suddenly felt self-conscious, standing in front of him in her underwear.

She had never been shy about her body. But this was Jake, and that was strange, and all she'd done was want and demand and push him around. She had to muffle a desire to laugh hysterically.

So instead, she said, "What should I do now?" in the surliest tone possible, and she put her hands on her hips and waited for him to make a move.

"I'm going to get condoms while there's still some sort of sense in me," he said, reaching for the drawer of his bedside table. "And why don't you take a seat?"

"So courteous."

"I feel like if I talk things through a bit, if I narrate, maybe we can figure it out. I probably don't have as much experience as you."

"What is that supposed to mean?" she asked tensely.

He took a breath. "It means I married the only person I ever had sex with." He paused with the unopened box of condoms in his hand. He said, "It means I feel self-conscious."

His frankness was bracing, adding another layer to the excitement she already felt. She did sit down on the bed then and pulled the sheet over her.

"Well, I feel self-conscious, too. That you're judging me. Because it's different for boys. I treat teenage girls, and it's still the same. The boys sleep around, and they're studs. The girls do it, and some idiot tells them their cooch smells like hot dog water."

"*Cooch*."

"Thank you, yes. I collect terms. Professional interest. I keep a spreadsheet of slang and euphemisms for vagina."

He shook his head. "I'd like to see your spreadsheet," he said, his voice a little strangled.

"I do know my way around a pivot table."

He put one hand around her ankle.

"You know, for a guy who says he's self-conscious, you're pretty bold."

"I was a jerk when I was a kid," he said, stroking his way up her leg. "And I'm certainly not perfect now. But I'm learning, and I'm working on it. I need to work on a lot of things. So, like I was saying, I am going to talk through this, and I'm going to trust you to tell me what's right for you. I'm going to need you to tell me how you feel. And when it feels good, I'll do it again, and keep doing it again and again right there until it's perfect."

He looked right into her eyes at that moment, and they both seemed to take a deep breath together.

"So tell me," he said. "Tell me what to do."

She shook her head. She took the hand that had been on her leg and brought it higher up, to the warm, soft skin inside her thigh.

His thumb moved as if to soothe her, but she was too stirred up, her blood too thick for this. She kissed him and rolled over him, and he plunged his hand deeper, past the warm cotton of her underwear, and he began to stroke between her legs.

"More of that," she said.

And he flipped her to her back, pausing only to remove the rest of her clothing, and he stroked again, his other hand reaching out.

They were attached that way, now. A crisscross of gazes and arms—hers on his chest, his cock, his on her breast, between her legs—each stroke bringing them closer together.

"I need to—"

"Get the condom. *Now.*"

He tore into it, his face looking almost relieved as he rolled it on. Almost.

Maybe it was wrong of her, but she couldn't help it. She took a moment to admire his cock with the rubber, almost translucent, stretched over it. She ran her finger over the snug band at the top and then cupped his balls.

He groaned.

She pushed him down on the bed, and even though her heart was beating so hard, her entire body hot and pulsing, she raised herself up slowly, took him in her hand, and rubbed him along herself.

"Sarah, please. Sarah."

She sat on her heels—onto him—in a hard slide, and her muscles gave an involuntary squeeze at the pressure of him. He groaned again and grasped her hips tight, his fingers telling her he wanted her to ride him even as he restrained himself.

She rose again and looked down at his cock sliding out of her, wet with her, and went down again. "I need—I need—"

His legs thrashed and his jaw tightened, but he put a palm against her mound, pushing into her as she moved on him, twisting his hand around as she leaned over to kiss him. "Yes, there," she said, and he did it again and again, just as he'd promised he would.

He pressed once more, and she could just feel it looping toward her as she leaned down to take his mouth in a sloppy kiss. He cried out, his teeth hitting her lip as his body jerked. But she was moaning, too, her hand slipping on his sweat-slicked chest onto the sheet below, and she felt her whole being stiffen before she broke apart and fell down, down onto him and let herself go limp.

CHAPTER SEVEN

He was probably dead, Jake thought, after a few minutes. That was the most likely explanation for how he felt. He wasn't tired. He could sense his body, but it was different. Tingling. He had just experienced all the feeling in the world, on his skin, in his vitals, all over his mind. And now he just *was*.

Sarah was draped over him, her breathing slowing down with his.

She rolled slowly off him, and the drag of her body letting go of his cock woke him and nearly sent his nerves over the edge again.

He looked down at the condom.

"It's broken," she said, slowly.

So many different expressions were flitting across her face right now. Her content had been chased away by disbelief. Annoyance. Exasperation. Fear.

He opened his mouth. He closed it again. "Sarah, are you on the pill? Are you allowed to use the pill after—after your treatment?"

"I'm on the pill."

"I mean, I doubt anything will happen—"

She held up her hand. "Believe me, I know the risks. And pregnancy is the least of my worries."

A pause.

"Right, I don't have any—you know. I just want to—"

"Don't try to soothe me right now. It's fine. I'm also clean. It's fine."

"Okay."

"Maybe go get rid of the rest of that."

He rose.

"Agreeing with me to placate me also counts as soothing," she said, following him.

He shook his head. "Are you coming after me to hector me?"

"No, I'm going to use the bathroom to prevent the risk of UTI. Then I'm going to go back to bed to hector you from atop a pillow."

He blinked, took a deep breath, and tried not to glance down.

"Oh my god, you're turned on by that," she said, her gaze going to his groin.

"Something about the combination of pillow and you yelling at me," he said helplessly.

She relaxed, her whole face and body softening, and she went on her tiptoes and kissed him. He grabbed her with his free hand and pulled her closer to him. But after a minute, she wriggled away. He was happy to see that she was as breathless as he was.

They ended up not going back to bed. They took showers—separately. By the time he got out, she was in the kitchen with the dog, drinking something green.

She pushed a glass toward him. "I raided your fridge. It's called a Makes Me Stronger smoothie."

"Fun name."

"Well, the full name is That Which Doesn't Kale Me Makes Me—"

He took a big gulp and it was … pretty good.

His relief must have shown on his face, because she laughed before taking another sip.

He focused on making sure that Mulder had enough food and water. They were hungry, so he made eggs and toast, and she sat at the kitchen table and laughed at the dog.

He liked it. So of course he had to go and spoil the moment.

"Would it be so bad even if you did turn out to be pregnant?" he asked.

She paused with a fork to her mouth, and her body stiffened.

But he'd already started. He might as well say his piece. "I mean, we both work. We're both mature—well, over thirty. And we're not terrible people. I'm just saying it wouldn't be the worst thing for us. Right now. I know you have sensitivities about this stuff—"

"Sensitivities." She laughed humorlessly. "We are not going to talk about having children right now."

"Well, you were unhappy about the condom. It's not unreasonable to choose this particular time to say that it really wouldn't be the worst thing in the world in the unlikely event that it did happen."

"I think that this might be the very, absolutely worst time in the world, actually, Jake. I think it might be the worst time in the world because we just had sex for the first time—and possibly for the last. And because I clearly don't want to talk about it right now."

"I'm not saying this because I want kids right now. I'm just trying to reassure you that I wouldn't shirk my responsibility."

He was messing this up. He was ruining it at every turn. He was supposed to know how to talk to people about hard things— he was supposed to know what to say, but he couldn't say the right thing to Sarah.

"And I'm trying to tell you that I know my job as an ob/gyn. I understand how to take a contraceptive pill and administer an emergency contraceptive pill."

"I'm not questioning your competence. You know way more about it than I do. I mean you're a doctor and a woman. I just … I just want to point out that I would be there and it wouldn't be a terrible mistake."

"For you."

"For me. Yes."

Another pause.

"Despite the fact that Winston would probably accuse me of entrapping you. And my parents would probably believe him. Your dad would probably say so, too."

He pressed his lips together. "I can handle Winston."

Again, it was the wrong thing to say.

"No, I'd have to handle Winston. And everyone else. No matter how good your intentions are, you can't shield me."

"That's because their words still hurt you."

He regretted that as soon as it left his lips.

"Of course they do."

She finished her drink and started to rinse out the glass.

"I'll do that."

She didn't answer.

"You have good intentions, Jake. But I am so tired of being put in this position for doing nothing wrong. In the end, everyone believes what they want to believe—and you are like my family in so many ways. Just the way you automatically had us co-parenting after one time in bed—the way you insist on talking this through now. We've known each other a long time. And because of that, I think you fall into old ways of thinking with me. Listen to the way you were talking. Like you had to save my virtue. . And then you had a future planned out. You were willing to raise a kid with me just a few minutes ago."

"I shouldn't have brought it up. But it was so nice afterward, and I kept thinking of how it would be great if it would go on."

God, could he get any more pathetic? Sarah was angled away from him, and all he wanted to do was grab her and kiss her. Instead he ran his hands through his hair. "No, you're right. I stop thinking I can save you but I'm trying. I'm really trying."

"I don't have time to guide you through your newfound enlightenment, Jake. And that's the other thing: you were still married not that long ago and ... I can't be a placeholder woman."

He growled. "You're not and you know it. And it's not like you aren't as vulnerable as I am right now."

They held each other's eyes for a moment. Sarah looked down first. "Yeah. That's the problem, I guess. I'm not over everything. I'm still battling memories of what my parents did to me. Our pasts are too intertwined. I'm not ready for this. Like you said, I'm weak right now."

"I said you were vulnerable, not weak. Sometimes, when those cracks are showing is when you can start something."

"No. I'm not ready."

Her voice was so small. He had never heard her this way before, and it hurt.

She put the glass away. She went upstairs and he followed her. She started to put on the rest of her clothing.

"Let me at least drive you home," he said.

"I'm calling a cab," she said, her phone in hand. "I can't talk about this right now. I need some time."

And with Jake and Mulder trailing her like a pair of ghosts, she went back down the stairs. She leaned down to pat the dog, then walked out the door.

• • •

"And then he told me that it wouldn't be the worst thing if I got pregnant."

Helen nodded. She was driving today.

Sarah and Helen were secretly scoping out a yoga retreat for Petra's shower-ette, or bachel-ower, or whatever the hell they were going to end up calling it.

Helen, as usual, had refused to turn on the GPS, and now they seemed to be lost.

Sarah told herself that that was why she felt tense. "Listen, do you want me to just check the map on my phone?"

"It wasn't the best thing to say, given your history. But I am having a hard time condemning him for it. And maybe I admire that he yet lives after arguing with the great Sarah Soon, that he was trying, in his very awkward way, to take responsibility for the whole thing."

"*I* can be responsible for my own body."

"I know that, Sarah. He wasn't saying you weren't. He wanted to talk practicalities, and you went in with all those feelings."

"Feelings? I was *very practical.* And need I remind you we slept together *once? Once.*"

"But it was different for you—he's different from the men you've been with before. He had you thinking things even before you had sex with him. He started out at the next level, Sarah. You went into it with more than you usually do."

Sarah sighed, but she wasn't able to deny it.

"You've known him a really long time."

"That's the problem. I don't know him and I do. He doesn't quite look the same anymore. He doesn't sound the same. But then he suddenly he does, and it's terrible and comforting and really confusing at the same time."

Helen pulled off the freeway and made her way to a gas station. Sarah surreptitiously pulled out her phone and Googled the directions while Helen spoke to the attendant.

"You've got to learn to trust that other people—people other than you—are capable of doing things," Helen said when the car starting moving again.

"I can't believe you're taking his side."

"I'm not. I meant me. We've arrived, and we didn't need you to check your phone for directions."

Helen pulled into a long, circular drive and shut off the ignition. They'd arrived at the yoga center.

Sarah sat in the car for a second. "Oh come on, you have to admit you got a little, tiny bit lost," she called after Helen's departing figure.

Helen flipped her the bird.

Sarah had to agree grudgingly that a day of spa and yoga on these serene, green grounds seemed like a good choice. They passed a gleaming rock garden and a fragrant patch of herbs filled with enthusiastic bees and butterflies. A quietly ebullient young woman showed them a sunlit studio and a massage room. She spoke about snail extract facial masks, and they had an animated conversation about juicing.

"I like it," Sarah said when they got back to the car, "but do you think it might be a little pricey? Especially if we invite Petra's mom, her sister, her sister's partner, and Joanie. Would they pay their own way?"

"I don't know. I think we're going to have to check up on this stuff. This is the first wedding-type thing I've ever had to plan. At least Petra isn't having bridesmaids, so we don't have to spring for dresses. We just basically have to show up. I want to do something that Petra will love, though. She refs all of our fights, lets us sleep on her couch. She holds us together."

"That's a pretty thankless role. We should have started thinking about this months ago."

"We were busy."

Sarah was silent. She had been sick.

"Are you worried about money?" Helen asked.

"Well, I'm still working enough to cover ob/gyn malpractice insurance and student loans and, you know, my kale habit."

Barely.

Helen didn't say much as she pulled back onto the freeway.

"For so much of my life, I've been so focused. Completing med school. Getting through my residency. Going into practice. So, I guess I needed a breather. But I feel like I dropped the ball—on my patients, on my friendships, on the things that matter."

"Sarah."

"But at the same time, I can't seem to make myself start again or be the same way again. It's like something in me has frozen up. Usually I can talk myself through a setback. When I didn't match to the hospital I applied for, when I didn't get the rotation I wanted, I worked hard with what I was given—I reorganized myself and thrived. But this time, this … illness had almost nothing to do with me—it's not even really a setback, right? I got sick, and it wasn't about my diet, and it wasn't about exercise or sleep or stress or how damn hard I worked. It wasn't about anything I could control—"

"Or anything you could blame yourself for, Sarah. Isn't that really the issue?"

Sarah slumped in her seat. Did Jake really deserve her anger? He had been nervous. It was his first time with her—with anyone after his wife. And yet, in his clumsy, misguided way, he had been trying to comfort her and tell her that he was there for her. And she had yelled at him. He had been trying so hard to be a good person, and she had run off because—because his care and immediate acceptance was frightening to her.

Sarah scrubbed her face with her hands. "We have got to stop having earnest conversations in the car."

"Believe me, it's better this way. If one of us is driving, we can't look each other deep in the eyes."

"Just for that, I'm going to eat the Pop-Tarts you have stashed in the glove compartment."

"Knowing how you feel about simple carbs, eating Pop-Tarts would be as much a punishment for you as for me."

Sarah slumped in the seat. "Fuck off."

"I love you, too."

CHAPTER EIGHT

Jake was used to fielding nerve-wracking after-hours phone calls. But the one he was listening to right now was making him pinch his forehead in frustration.

His father, the Reverend Telly Li.

His father wasn't terrifying. He was slight and serious looking. His glasses were always a little askew. He always had an absent-minded smile. Most of the time, he looked eager—eager to please, to tell people what was on his mind, to just be in the room.

But as a voice over the telephone, the Reverend Doctor Telly Li was a lot more disconcerting.

"The conference is Tuesday through Friday. I know it's short notice, but I wanted to see how you are doing."

Unspoken was the fact that they hadn't seen each other since Jake's divorce was finalized. The reverend was dismayed, to say the least. The thought of dealing with his father now—now especially because of the split, and because of Sarah—made him tense. Jake made a note to get an extra set of sheets. And a new pillow.

Mulder gave a sharp bark.

"What's that?"

"It's my dog."

A pause. "You have a dog now?"

And there it was. Slightly mistrustful.

Jake didn't take the bait. "Her name is Mulder. You'll meet her Tuesday, I guess."

"Wednesday night, actually. I'm just surprised that you are taking on extra responsibility for a pet now that you're alone. You have to walk a dog."

"Yes, I may have heard something about that."

"Your job is sometimes time consuming. You have emergencies."

"There will always be emergencies in life. Besides, I have a walker and a house with a yard now."

A pause.

"That's true," the reverend said slowly.

At least he didn't say something about swing sets and children. When Jake was still married, the reverend had pestered him to move to a house with a garden and lawn and spoke to Ilse about grandkids. But now it seemed he was going to let it pass. And to his credit, the reverend had given up on trying to get Jake and Ilse back together. For a while, his father had emailed and talked and sent newspaper clippings and email forwards on how to save a marriage. He'd even driven down suddenly, intent on giving them a sex talk.

Luckily Ilse had not been there.

Well, at least there wasn't much to clean up, Jake thought, looking around at his nearly empty house.

The reverend's arrival was going to put a crimp in his plans to woo Sarah. Or not woo Sarah and just be cool and get to know her like a stranger would. She had at least texted him back yesterday, accepting his apology, but the reverend's presence would be a painful reminder for her of all the things they had and hadn't been to each other.

• • •

The reverend arrived on Wednesday night, as promised, wearing a short-sleeved dress shirt and polished shoes. His hair was a little grayer, and his glasses seemed greasy. He didn't chatter as much as he usually did, but otherwise, things seemed much the same as they had been for the last twenty or so years. The reverend was consistent—he had been almost strenuously consistent even after Jake's mother died after a short battle with breast cancer when Jake was nine.

It was late enough that they both went to bed fairly soon after his arrival.

Instead of ceding his slightly bigger bedroom to his father, Jake showed him the guest room. Not that his father cared. Without preamble, the reverend sat on the edge of the bed. Maybe he began to pray.

His father always looked vulnerable. Jake had forgotten that. Another thing that hadn't changed.

Jake closed the door and left his father to his murmurings.

Jake's Thursday started early, early in the morning with a phone call from his school. One of the special education students had been reported missing by her foster family. She had been in class on Wednesday.

It turned out that the student had gotten into a car accident and was afraid to face her foster parents. She had spent the night at a friend's house. But halfway through the night, she realized she didn't feel well, so she'd gone to the emergency department. She was still in the waiting room when they tracked her down.

In the past, Jake had sometimes wondered as he shuttled to and from hospitals if he'd run into Sarah there. But he wasn't lucky this time.

By the time Jake had finished visiting the student and talking to the foster parents, the girl's teachers, doctors, and CPS, it was late. His father was still out. Oddly enough, the table held a box of donuts from Voodoo. Jake could well imagine an ecclesiastical conference that included a stop at a hipster pastry shop. Had they stood in line wearing their collars? He peeked inside. His father had ordered a donut with chocolate frosting and a vanilla pentagram. Jake stuffed it into his mouth immediately. He hadn't had lunch, after all.

Halfway through the third (and probably last) bite, he realized his dog was not begging for donuts—because she was nowhere to be found.

He checked the backyard. Nothing. The basement door was shut tight, and there was no one down there. His bedroom was empty, the hastily thrown-back covers from this morning still half-hanging off his bed. He remembered the disarray that sleeping with Sarah had left. And now, here he was sharing quarters with a person who had preached a pointed sermon about wayward teens and the evils of premarital sex not three days after Sarah had been caught with that boy.

Now, of course, Jake knew that the whole thing had been a tempest in a teapot. But everything Sarah did—that he did—back then had been magnified and scrutinized because they were so visible even when they just wanted to shrink into the background. Sarah was vilified even though earlier that same year, the basketball team had decorated their lockers with condoms, and Sheryl What's-her-name had gotten pregnant. Blowjobs in the bleachers, wild parties in the woods—he couldn't remember the names of classmates who'd happily participated in all that fairly normal teenaged stuff. But Sarah had been caught with her shirt off *once*, and it had stuck. The community had slut-shamed her— even the tiny Asian population of Laketon and her parents. It was almost ridiculous, especially now that he saw it in the context of his training and because he worked with kids who had to grapple with much harsher realities. But the instance had repercussions, good and bad, for Sarah's life.

He heard the door open and the *click, click* of Mulder's paws on the bare hallway floor. "Oh, you're back," his dad said—guiltily?— when Jake took the leash from his dad's hand.

The reverend looked a little sweaty under his shirt, and Mulder had loped off to the kitchen to slurp up some water.

"You were at the park?" Jake asked, frowning.

"You have chocolate in your beard," his dad said, avoiding the question.

"I wasn't expecting you back till later. You usually go out to dinner with your colleagues and all that. Catch up on God stuff, gossip about the latest theology scandals, you know."

"Mmm."

The reverend shrugged and passed Jake to shut himself in the bathroom. There was a grass stain on his short-sleeved dress shirt.

Mulder passed out in a corner of the kitchen. Judging from her happy sleep and the dry leaves in her coat, she'd been playing outdoors for a while.

Jake was getting an odd feeling about his dad's visit.

"I could make dinner," Jake called.

Jake wasn't really in the mood to probe his dad's behavior, but the reverend wasn't a romp-in-the-park-and-roll-around-to-get-grass-stains kind of guy. Jake's instincts were on alert.

"Let's go out to eat! Let's try something different!" the reverend said.

His dad never wanted to go out for food. The reverend's position as a preacher in a tiny church in a rural region with only a small population of Chinese people hadn't been enough to support him and a family, so his father also worked as a bookkeeper. Money had sometimes been tight. They never ate out.

"Dad, is there really a conference?"

"There really is a conference." A pause. "I just didn't attend."

Jake took a breath—and decided to change the subject. His family counseling professor would have disapproved. "What do you feel like eating?" he said, getting out his phone.

"I don't know! Something different!"

"Yes, you said that."

His dad threw up his hands. "Something interesting and exciting! This is a big city!"

Jake shook his head.

They went to a Korean taco stand, and then they got crème brûlée flavored cotton candy, which, despite his father's alarming new carnival-like sense of whimsy, was probably too ambitious. They both ended up abandoning it. His father saw a juice truck, though, and enthusiastically ordered the biggest, greenest juice he could find. He was now sitting on a park bench, sipping it eagerly and talking to one of the tattooed hipsters sitting next to him about the durability of Doc Martens boots.

Kale juice reminded Jake of Sarah. The sheets reminded him of Sarah. If he wasn't careful, pretty soon he'd think the birds were chirping her name. Greg would have called him a wuss for pining for a woman he'd slept with once—for pining after a girl since high school, since junior high, since long before that really.

Greg could be an asshole. But he was back with his girlfriend and happier than ever.

"I've seen Sarah Soon in town a few times," he said to his dad.

He didn't know why he brought it up, especially because, he realized with a painful throb, he wasn't sure that she had forgiven him, despite the text. But there was an unexpectedly deep vein of yearning in him lately, and he just couldn't stop excavating more and more of it.

"Sarah. Sarah Soon? How is she?"

His father said it rather doubtfully, as if he were expecting news that Jake had found her sleeping in a trash can. Or maybe that was Jake's own defensive projection. He found himself saying, "She is amazing. She's done great things with her life, just like I knew she would. She's only gotten stronger and stronger."

His father laughed. "She was pretty strong-willed to begin with, as I recall."

It probably wasn't a compliment. Or maybe it was. Sarah would have seen it as one.

He considered his eager, awkward, outgoing father. In a way, he was deeply conservative—but that word was wrong. It was too simple, too evocative of pursed-lip white men and ladies wearing suits and hats. There was something joyless about the word. Jake's dad wasn't joyless. There had been hard years after Jake's mom died. His dad had come to the States from Taiwan to go to Union Theological College on a scholarship. He was a fixture in Laketon. He was friends with the other two church heads—the frowning Catholic priest, the jolly Baptist minister—and when all three went to the bar together, people usually tried to come up a punch line about them.

In the pulpit, his dad was clear, organized, and forceful. Jake's gradual loss of faith had also been a loss of his sense of his father as a man to be admired and followed. In the last five years, he had stopped believing and going to church. And until Jake's divorce, his father had convinced himself that Jake was going through a phase.

He wasn't. Although now, apparently the reverend was experiencing his own struggles. "There have been some changes in my life, son," his father said. "Ever since you left, probably. But it came to a head when you and Ilse—well, at least that's when I recognized it. I know, I know, your divorce doesn't affect me directly," he said when Jake started to speak, "but I got the sense of where did the time go? And I looked up and I was in this town and our church was getting smaller, and for the first time in a long time, I asked myself why I was still in Laketon trying to hold this congregation together. I prayed to God for answers and I didn't find any."

His dad sighed. "There was a conference today. And there's more tomorrow. And I was ready to go and I just didn't. I drove around Portland. I went to Powell's and hid for a while."

"Are you having a spiritual crisis, Dad?"

"That's an interesting question. No. At least I don't think so. But I am recognizing that I feel powerless in a way I haven't since your mother died. Or maybe I've been that way since your mother died and I didn't know it because I didn't … well, I just didn't give myself the time. Also, I'm thinking about getting remarried," he added.

"Wait. What? How? How is that the logical conclusion to those sets of sentences?"

His father shrugged, and Jake found the anger that he'd been holding in check bubble up. *This is not the time.* When he was younger, Jake functioned as his father's cleanup crew—finishing the dishes that his dad left in the sink, turning out all the lights in the house, making sure his dad ate. After all that had happened lately, Jake didn't want his father to lean on him. But there he was.

"After your mom died, I wish I could say I found great consolation in the Bible. But I found great consolation in you."

Jake shook his head.

"That sounds unhealthy, but it was how I coped. Maybe it is, as you say, a spiritual crisis, because I didn't seek comfort in God. I always did better talking with people than I did with theology. I'm sorry, Jacob. I shouldn't be burdening you with this."

"Who is this person you want to marry?"

"Her name is Judy. She's a pediatrician in Kennewick, originally from China. She's a bit younger. She wants babies, of course."

Jake nodded and tried to absorb the information.

"We haven't really had a discussion about the future," his father added. "But she must be expecting a wedding and children because we are dating—I know it's not how you kids do this nowadays. When young people date, they just go out and there is no guarantee that it will lead to marriage. But I'm old fashioned and I'm alone. And now you're alone, too. Except maybe you are dating Sarah?"

Of course his dad had pierced right through to it.

"I'd like to. If she'll have me."

He and his father had both been half-lying to each other and themselves for so long, and now all of those thoughts were so knotted and messy that Jake couldn't even distinguish his own or his father's feelings—whether it was that he felt sorry for Jake's solitude or doubtful that Sarah would ever settle down, Jake wasn't sure.

"Maybe while I'm in town," his father continued after a silence, "it's a good idea to go out to dinner with her. I haven't seen her in a long time. Maybe something like this." He gestured around the food trucks. "Does she like artisan hot dogs?"

"I'm not sure how any of this would go over."

"I remember her when she was a little girl," his father said absently. "Your mother loved her. So cute and lively. But what a handful when she grew up."

Jake felt his mouth tighten. "Actually, Dad, she was a pretty normal teen girl."

Ignoring him, his father continued, "Listen, I will keep an open mind. I need to learn to do that."

But his dad's open mind wasn't what Jake was worried about. Jake wanted to see Sarah again. But he wanted to do it on his terms—without the shadow of his father. But when was that ever going to happen?

Hell, he wasn't even sure that she would agree to see him for all that she was now answering his texts. Could he blame her? Years later, the reverend was still holding that one small event over her.

And still, Jake knew. He knew he was going to ask Sarah to join them, because he wanted to see her. It was an excuse—and maybe because he knew plotting and planning wasn't going to cut it with her. It was time for him to just want and need and to tell her.

He had to see her.

CHAPTER NINE

Sarah probably would not have caved to Jake if she hadn't been talking to her mom just minutes before he showed up at her door.

But her mom did not telephone often. For years, she did not speak to her daughter. Sarah and her dad chatted sometimes, but he didn't reach out unless Sarah left a message. Then eventually, Fai Soon started calling again. And maybe that was worse than the silence. Those strained talks had a terrible softening effect on Sarah: sometimes it was like being soaked in a warm soothing bath, and sometimes it was like having a meat mallet taken to her insides. Usually it was both in one conversation. Either way, her mom's careful voice over the receiver inquiring how she was and awkwardly delivering news about extended family always led to a final blow: asking how she was doing, as if she expected Sarah to have screwed up. Again.

"You brother said we should check on you," her mother said. "He said you might not have been letting on you were sicker than you said you were."

Sarah felt that weight of accusation again. She *had* been taking care of her health, before and after the surgery.

"I'm fine," Sarah said more firmly than she felt.

The only way to deal with her family was to sound like she knew what she was doing—to sound like she didn't need them or, more important, want to need them. Because while they had once given love, they also doled out hurt. If she were trapped in a cave with water coming higher and higher, she would adopt exactly the same tone with her mother that she was taking now, even as she panicked.

"I'm fully recovered. I have gone in for all my follow-ups, and as long as I continue to be vigilant, I don't anticipate any problems."

Speaking in English and using her doctor voice tended to both comfort and stymie her mother.

"You didn't tell us it was cancer."

"No, I didn't. How did you find out?"

"Jake's dad told us."

There was a long silence—which was typical of most of their relationship for the last fifteen or so years.

Her mother finally said, "The reverend says he's in town for a conference. If you see him, take him out to dinner."

She hung up.

It was no coincidence that her mother was checking up on her, then. A double whammy of Winston and the reverend. And now Jake was standing at her door, in jeans and a t-shirt that molded tautly to his lean body when the wind kicked up.

It was completely unfair.

They might have stood for a minute, looking at each other. But Mulder, not believing an invitation was needed, bounded inside, and Jake ... well, Jake simply let go of her leash. His eyes crinkled.

So. Completely. Unfair.

Sarah turned and stalked to the kitchen, aware that he had closed the door gently and was following her. She started chopping some greens into teeny-tiny pieces.

"You have good knife skills," he said, folding his long limbs under the counter.

Out of the corner of her eye, she assessed the sleek muscles of his shoulders—a little loose around the middle where his golden skin would be making small hard ridges, a topographic delight that had been traveled by her eager fingers. Involuntarily, her hands tightened.

She put her eyes back on the cutting board.

"Thanks for letting me in," Jake said, after a pause.

"What's going on?"

He took a deep breath. "My dad's in town. He wants to have dinner with you. And I want to see you again—although not under these circumstances. But I'll take what I can get."

"Not that I'm trying to help your cause, but having your dad in the room is not likely to make me think more kindly of you."

"We'd be a study in contrasts."

"You told him about the cancer."

"Was it a secret?"

"No, I guess not."

She turned to get some eggs from the fridge. When she turned back, he was still watching her from under the dark flop of hair—intensely and seriously and carefully. The way he'd always watched her, she had to confess to herself. When she was younger, she'd told herself it was because he was waiting for her to say something outrageous or make a mistake. But that wasn't it. That had never been it. After all, she'd watched him back, in her own way. And maybe she was the one hoping he'd screw up.

"I also told him we had been seeing each other," he said.

She cracked an egg into a bowl. "*Had been* is the operative phrase here."

"Well, that's true."

"Did you say we were present tense seeing each other?"

"No, I didn't. But it's not because I don't think of you all the time. Or want you all the time."

His voice had suddenly dipped low—as low as the hot spot between her thighs—and an abrupt scrape of the stool brought him nearer.

She jumped a little and dropped an egg on the countertop. As she watched, the egg meandered toward him, uncracked. He picked it up with one hand, and with the other, he pulled her wrist to him and tucked the egg into her palm, closing her fingers around it.

They stood there for a moment, her hand in both of his, gingerly holding the egg.

She pulled herself out of his grasp.

"I like you, Jake. I always have, in a way. And I enjoyed the sex, a lot." She held up her hands as he moved toward her again, his face intent. "Okay, down boy. If you get any closer, you're going to end up in the omelet."

He stopped, because he always did listen to her.

She sobered. "But it is not my job to make you a better person. I do not owe you, and I don't have time. And I am most definitely not going to be your fake girlfriend like we're in some kind of zany plot to fool your father that you're doing just fine and get him off your back."

"You are most definitely not the person I'd choose as my fake girlfriend, Sarah."

"Thanks."

"That's a compliment. You're real, and you aren't intimidated by the reverend. You won't take his bullshit, and you call me on mine. But I'm asking you to go because I want you with me. I'm tired of not seeing you, and I'm at the point where I frankly don't care what the conditions are. I don't even care that I'm pressuring you. Come with me as a friend. Come with me because you have things to tell the reverend about the person you've become. Come with me to tell him off. Come for whatever reason. But sit with me. Talk to me. Be with me. You'll see it won't be the worst thing you've ever had to do—far from it."

"This is unusually self-interested of you."

"You sound like you like that."

"To a point. I'm really not likely to jump you if you start quoting Ayn Rand."

"When are you most likely to jump me, then?"

She huffed out a laugh, but her body had flushed all over. "I have a knife," she said.

"Hippocratic oath."

"Why does everyone invoke that like a talisman against me?"

"Because it is. You're a small, powerful, creature with a blade, and people need to be careful around you."

"Be careful around me or be careful of me?"

"Maybe a little of both."

She put the knife down. She sat down. "I don't want to go," she said in a small voice.

This time he did pull her to him, and he felt so warm and comforting that she didn't stop herself from burying her face in his chest.

He sighed. "I shouldn't ask you, then. I also thought this might be a step to change things for you. You'd see that people are different now. Or that they can't hurt you anymore."

She breathed in the laundry soap smell of his shirt and squeezed her eyes shut. "That is such bullshit, Jake." Then she added very quietly, "I'll go." She stepped away from him. "Besides, my mom just asked me to."

Jake watched her. He was pleased and maybe surprised. "I'm surprised that you'd do this for her."

"Yes, well, it's complicated. But she'll owe me."

They were both still for a couple of beats, listening to the dog's tail make a *thwump* against the floor.

"I still don't know if I forgive you," Sarah added.

Jake kissed her forehead, so light. It only made her want more.

"I don't know if you should yet."

He snapped for a suddenly obedient Mulder, and they let themselves out of her house.

• • •

"So, uh, who picked this place?" Sarah asked a few hours later, watching their server depart.

That server, Elspeth, who was decidedly white, was wearing a mandarin-collared jacket. She also had decorative chopsticks— one with little fan pendants and one with the double happiness symbol—stuck in her hair. Maybe it was the restaurant's version of flare. Maybe Elspeth would keep collecting chopsticks until her bun was bristling with so much heavy metal that it could be used as a mace.

"I chose it," the reverend answered cheerfully. "I looked it up on one of those websites. They're known for their *nouveau riche and stinky tofu*. I haven't had stinky tofu since my last trip to Taiwan seven years ago."

"*Nouveau riche and stinky tofu?*" she mouthed at Jake.

"It's made of fermented scrapings from gold ingots maybe?" he whispered, leaning close to her ear.

The reverend's eyes flashed from behind the menu, taking in the sight of Sarah and his son lip to ear. Sarah felt herself blush. What the fuck was that about? But instead of jerking away as she once may have done, she felt herself lean in and murmur back, "It's made of the crackling skin of desperate old misers."

"I think I read that book. Is it by Amy Tan?"

Sarah shivered as his voice skittered low across her skin.

"Children," the reverend interrupted, putting down the menu, "what do you think we should get?"

Elspeth returned. "So, let me tell you a little bit about what we have today. Everything is family style, and if you order the tasting menu, we prefer that everyone at the table do the same. Today, our chef Neville Dobley-Howe is offering a selection of buns three ways: pork belly with cherry reduction, a lotus seed puree, and our house special crystal wheatgrass and water spinach."

"I think we'll probably need a minute—or like, maybe another century of post-colonialism," Sarah muttered.

"Of course, take your time," Elspeth sang. "May I take your drink orders?"

"Should I have a Taiwanese Mai Tai or a Ginseng Sling?" the reverend asked.

Sarah stifled a little groan.

"We also have a selection of microbrews from Taipei," Elspeth said, turning the reverend's menu over in his hands.

"Oh, thank you. Let's try this," he said, pointing and squinting.

Elspeth looked around at Jake and Sarah, who shook their heads at alcohol. The kids were not here to play, it seemed.

There was a small silence. Sarah said, "Have you noticed that we're the only Asian people here?"

"It's a white people restaurant," the reverend agreed easily. "That's why they can charge higher prices."

He scratched the inlaid table with his fingernail. "All this decoration is maybe a bit much, though."

"It's verging on racist."

The reverend laughed. "I'm not offended by it. I'm old enough and have lived here long enough that any remotely positive attention to our culture is flattering—and a relief."

"Even if it's caricature? And there aren't any actual Chinese people involved in the making of the whole restaurant? And what is a Mai Tai doing on the menu of a Chinese—faux Chinese—restaurant?"

"The restaurant is supposed to be mostly Taiwanese," the reverend said—maybe a little condescendingly.

It was galling, but she blushed anyway. She knew the difference between the two—God knows it had been pointed out frequently in her childhood. Even though Jake's dad and her parents could stumble along in Mandarin together, that didn't mean that they didn't snipe about the others' ways.

The reverend added, "I heard Taiwanese is becoming fashionable, what with *Fresh off the Boat* and Jeremy Lin and all. Are there a lot of Taiwanese people in Portland?"

Sarah stayed silent—she didn't know for sure.

Jake shook his head. "Mostly Cantonese."

After a short silence, Sarah said, "Well, as for Taiwanese being fashionable, that's weird for—I don't even know how to describe it—for someone's country of origin to be fashionable. I'm not going to argue with you about whether we're all God's precious babies after all. But it's weird."

"Maybe we should just have a drink here and leave," Jake suggested.

But the reverend reached over and stayed him—almost touched him. Jake seemed to flinch away.

"I want to see what the hot places in Portland are"—a definite wince from Jake—"and I want my stinky tofu. After all that, you may lecture us, Sarah."

"I don't want to sit here smiling so that white people can look over at us and decide that this place *must be* good because there are real Asian people eating here," Sarah grumbled.

But she was fighting a losing battle against her hollow stomach and, well, guilt. Despite her differences with the reverend, he looked older and tired, and she'd been trained to be forgiving— and he was a minister and her parents' friend. He had experienced more blatant terrible things when he'd first come to America. He was wrong, but was she going to push it right now?

She was already planning her nasty Yelp review for later, though.

"We could hire ourselves out as *those* Asian people who legitimize a place if our lucrative careers don't work out," Jake said.

She snorted. "I might have to take you up on that."

"Me, too," said the reverend, a little too seriously.

Jake smirked. She raised her brows at Jake, and he gave his head a slight shake.

Something was definitely wrong between the two of them. Now that she'd relaxed into her indignation, she noticed the currents between father and son. In fact, Jake seemed to be avoiding his father a lot.

Elspeth came back, and the reverend decided to go for the eight-course tasting menu. Sarah thought about protesting, but she decided she was tired. *Might as well see what Neville Doogie-Howser can do.* Soon, a sour plum powder and watermelon amuse-bouche appeared at the table. The reverend closed his eyes and folded his hands, saying a small prayer at the table. Jake did not join in, she noticed. He waited with her, not looking at her, and when his father finished, he took a sip of his water.

By the time the bussers had laid down three bowls of what appeared to be jellyfish salad, the reverend was red-faced and a little garrulous. "Did my son tell you that I'm thinking about getting married? Judy's thirty-nine."

Jake's potential new stepmother was just five years older than them.

"Tell us about her," Sarah said, genuinely curious.

Jake, on the other hand, may have turned a little green. But she was still annoyed with him for bringing her to this dinner, and she was going to needle him for just a little longer.

"She wants a family. She's a pediatrician. You would have a lot in common. Or maybe not. I guess you deal with the stuff at the beginning, and she deals with the end result. I think I would like more children. But I'm old. I was hoping for grandchildren actually."

Nothing subtle there. No wonder Jake was unhappy. He was probably wishing he'd ordered a drink by now.

"You wish he were still married to Ilse?"

"Yes. You know I do. This breaks my heart."

"Dad. Ilse's getting married in a month."

Sarah did not like this at all. "What about Jake? What about how he feels? How did their marriage turn into something that is all about you?"

"Everything we do affects the entire community, Sarah."

"There you go again."

"What does that mean?"

"It means that you take these things that happen to Jake, or me, or any one of your flock, and you tell them they can't do them because they have to be a *good example*. This isn't about God or community. This is about how people perceive you, your feelings, and how you think your life should be ordered."

"Jake needs to set an example. He is my son."

"Jake has spent his entire life trying to be a good person, and not just in the coaching Little League and organizing food drives way. Remember how he'd hand deliver groceries to Ms. Johns after his shift at the store?"

Jake said softly, "But I didn't defend you when you needed a friend, Sarah."

"You can't help everyone, Jake."

She turned to the reverend. "Anyway, you probably never noticed them, because Jake just does this without making a big deal out of it. But you take his divorce—which isn't even a reflection on him, isn't even bad so much as it is sad and painful for him—and you give him a hard time and hint at how he ought to still be married to Ilse. He has been a good example for his entire life. Why instead of a paragon and representative of the community can't you just let him be a person?"

The reverend pressed his lips together. And then, to her horror, his face seemed to just collapse softly.

"I struggle all the time," he said. "And lately, I wonder if I'm doing the right thing. If I can continue to counsel people when my son's life is unhappy. If I can bring more children into the world when I don't know anything. I'm older. I'm getting old. And instead of growing into wisdom, instead of finding myself settled, I find I have more questions all the time—more questions about myself most of all. If I've done the right things. I tried to have God guide me."

Sarah slid down in the booth. She was arguing with a drunk clergyman in a pseudo-Asian restaurant, and her maybe-boyfriend was probably angry with her. This was definitely not what her mother had in mind when she'd told Sarah to take the reverend out. Could the evening get worse?

"Dried shredded tuna," Elspeth sang as she put down the dish. "And this is our house special savory soy milk. You spoon a little bit on top and eat it together."

"We *know* how to eat it," Jake muttered.

"*Ell-Em-Kay* if you need anything else."

Jake leaned and whispered fiercely as if Sarah wouldn't hear, "Dad, pull yourself together. Do you need me to walk you to the bathroom?"

"I remember when Sarah was a baby, she had the brightest eyes and she would look so long and fixedly at everything. At first I thought it was strange in a child so small. And when she grew up and stayed that way—"

She was going to choke on her inappropriate laughter. She was going to choke on this dry-ass, thready, salty fish floss.

"*Dad.*"

The reverend stopped. He gulped a glass of water. "I seem to have gotten carried away."

He waved Jake off and toddled toward the back of the restaurant.

"Is he going to be okay?" Sarah asked. "I'm sorry. I don't—I mean, he's not a bad person."

"He tries hard, too."

"Don't we all."

Jake started to laugh. "It's true. We all try hard, Sarah. You attempt to be perfectly organized and on top of it. I try to do the right thing. The reverend keeps plugging away at our souls. And look at us, we're a mess."

Sarah started to smile tentatively. "You aren't mad at me? For making your dad get teary?"

"I knew you had it in you, Killer."

She did laugh at that.

After a minute, she added, "I didn't like the way he was putting so much on you."

"He blames himself for how I've turned out."

"You've turned out just goddamn fine. You've turned out great! You have some actual fucking self-respect, Jake. I am so angry that he can't see that."

"Maybe. I don't know. I don't know if it's on purpose, in any case. He doesn't react well to change."

"Well, that's true of a lot of us."

There were quiet for a minute.

"Maybe you should go find your dad."

"You'll stay, right? Even though he's embarrassed you? Even though I've put you in a crap situation?"

He took her wrist gently, and every nerve in her body shot to life, as if electrified. Her eyes found his inadvertently, and she couldn't move away. She didn't want to.

He let go.

He rubbed his forehead. "I mean, you should leave if you want."

"Dammit, Jake. Why don't you ever say what *you* want?"

"I want you," he said low. He wasn't even sitting as close anymore, but she felt the hot, dark waves coming off him. "I want you—I've wanted you all this time. Is that what you need to hear? Your mouth in particular fascinates me, especially when you get mad and try to defend me. I want you all the damn time always, and if we weren't out in public, I'd take you lying down on this inlaid table. With a lychee fruit nestled in your belly button."

She had leaned in to hear him, and now she drew back. She put her hands on the table so that they wouldn't shake. She wanted him, too, but now was not the time—which he knew. But she had pushed him, and even he seemed surprised at what had tumbled out of his mouth.

She tried to sound light. "Well, the last thing I need is for your dad to catch me with an Edible Arrangement in my navel." But she was blushing. She thought she'd given up blushing. "Anyway," she said, trying to brush it all off, "are you saying this stuff because he's here? Is this some scheme to piss him off? Is that why you brought me?"

He made an effort to recover. "Never doubt that fruit in your belly button is a good look for you."

She closed her eyes. His voice was warm, like a hand touching her in all the right places. She was going to die of embarrassment and sexual frustration right here in a dumb faux-Chinese restaurant. He ran his fingertips over her clenched fists. "I need to go check on my dad," he said in her ear. "I'd like you to stay. Please don't run off because we're terrible."

She drew in a shaky breath. "Why would I run? My fantasy date is men crying while I down artisanal soy milk."

She stayed, not that she thought it was a good idea. But Jake had been a mistake from the minute she met him again. And yet, how was it that now that he had walked away from the table, she missed him?

• • •

The rest of the evening had gone as well as it could, under the circumstances. The chef, Neville Longbottom, or whatever, had come out to chat with them. His father engaged him in a long discussion about the influences of Taipei street food. They even spoke a little in Taiwanese, which Jake understood, but Sarah didn't. For a moment while his father and the chef conversed, her brow furrowed deeply, and Jake knew in that moment that she wished in her dark inky heart that they'd all get food poisoning from the restaurant.

How bad did he have it that her spite was a turn on?

But when they got to the car, Jake turned to his dad.

"Dad, you have to stop with this with Sarah."

The reverend didn't feign ignorance. "She's an outspoken young woman."

"That is so dismissive. You've always been condescending of her and of me. She was right, you know, about that stupid restaurant."

Jake knew he was going against his training—he was maybe making his father's confusion worse. But his dad wasn't a student. And Jake was mad. Was the reverend really at a turning point if he could cling so much to his old opinions? How much more of a crisis was it than the usual dad wringing his hands?

"That chef knows more about Taiwanese food and culture than Sarah does—or you. You young people, you think you know everything. You have no idea what I went through when I moved here."

"You're right, I don't. But meanwhile you have a doctorate of divinity. You've studied a Western religion, but your faith and knowledge and experience get questioned all the time. People doubt you know how to pray, how to even read and interpret the Bible in English, let alone Greek. And since when has a non-Asian person ever shown up for your English services? But people are willing to shower this Neville Whatsit with praise and money because he worked in Taipei for a year and can serve us a Taiwanese breakfast for dinner? Sure, he has skills. So do you. And if the fact that you're treated differently even though you're an expert in your field isn't some deeply held bias, I don't know what is."

"Religion is not a restaurant."

"It's not. But it's still telling. And if you think that these so-called little things are unconnected to the bigger things happening right now, then maybe you need to look harder."

"Sarah is giving you these ideas."

"No, she isn't. It's all stuff I used to think growing up, but I didn't know how to put it into words. But I've been out in the world. I've seen the things my kids deal with, and I've had time to figure out my own mind. Our experiences are leading us to different conclusions, and I think that's why you're upset with me."

Silence.

"Anyway, you shouldn't blame Sarah. It was a mistake bringing her."

"I asked you to."

"I wanted to show her ... something. I don't even know what. But instead I probably just pushed her away more."

More silence. Clearly, his father didn't believe him—that all of these thoughts predated Sarah. They hadn't lived in the same house for more than fourteen years. They hadn't agreed for even longer, not that Jake had shared that information with him. But the longer they were apart, the more his father seemed to keep Jake suspended in the golden glow of amber. And maybe it was Jake's fault, because he just grunted instead of disagreeing with the reverend—maybe it was his fault that he'd done that with Ilse. Now he'd divorced Ilse. And he'd gotten close to Sarah. He wanted to be closer.

"Sarah was sick with cancer and she's recovered." A sidelong glance. "Is that why you're so interested in her?"

"What is that supposed to mean?"

Luckily they were stopped at a red light.

"You like to save people, Jake. In a lot of ways, you saved me."

"Stop saying that, Dad. Maybe the problem is that you keep saying that."

His father shrugged. Apparently, the conversation was over.

Later, when they got home, Jake couldn't sleep. Maybe it was the weirdly spiced soymilk or the matcha dessert. Or maybe it was his dad's words.

Perhaps Sarah had been right. She said herself that she was unsteady on her feet these days—not because she was still sick, but because her certainty in herself was shaken. And he was still feeling his way around the edges of his own life right now: He was trying to figure out what he liked to do in the quiet hours when he got home, trying to make sure he didn't work himself into a breakdown. He was finding places he liked to run or walk with Mulder, maybe even attempting to reacquaint himself with his friends. Maybe his dad had a point, too. It wouldn't be so strange that he would try and manage Sarah because he couldn't manage himself.

Sighing, he got up and pulled on a pair of shorts and a sweatshirt. Mulder followed him quietly, her nails clicking on the floor. He clipped her leash on, and they went outside into the cool night air.

He wanted to keep seeing Sarah. He'd practically extracted a promise from her that she'd see him next week after his father left. But maybe he was too screwed up himself.

Do something for yourself, she had told him. She wanted him to take what he wanted. She probably never expected that thing to be her.

CHAPTER TEN

It maybe wasn't nice to make her enemies cry, but then Sarah hadn't considered herself nice for over a decade. Besides, despite how she'd built the reverend up in her mind, he wasn't really the enemy. She didn't feel good about the encounter, but as the next day wore on, she didn't feel guilty about it, either. She started acting more like her old, whole, healthy self. She corrected Petra, yelled at a drug rep who was rude to Joanie, and gave the finger to Helen at least four times. At the end of the day, she had an appointment with one of her favorite patients.

"The test came back positive. You're pregnant." Sarah paused for a moment.

The young woman was silent.

Sarah glanced at the chart again, not that she needed to. Lena was a college student, but she'd been Sarah's patient when Sarah worked with ProntoDocs! at the mall. Lena had come to Sarah a couple of days ago because of a suspected yeast infection and asked casually about having a different test. Now she was back for the results.

"Was this a planned pregnancy?"

A short laugh from Lena.

"It's very early on," Sarah said gently. "At this point, pregnancies often fail."

"I can't. I can't have a baby right now. You understand, don't you? It was an accident. I want—I want a termination. I can't do this."

"I understand, Lena. I'd say the fetus is about eight weeks. Very early. You're just within the range for medical abortion—which is nine weeks. I'm going to give you the information on clinics, but basically if you do this, they'll administer mifepristone, and usually about twenty-four hours later, you'll take misoprostol at home. You'll need someone to bring you to the clinic and keep an eye on you at home because there'll be a lot of bleeding."

At Lena's look, she added, "It's fairly straightforward, and you don't have to remember all of this. I'll give you the information. You can always talk to me anytime, too, and ask more questions."

Sarah touched her arm and said gently, "It's a lot to take in, but you already suspected, didn't you?"

Lena nodded.

Sarah said, "I can call and make an appointment for you myself. It's very common and safe. But it's okay if you change your mind—you have the choice."

Lena didn't respond.

Sarah added gently, "You need to do the right thing for yourself. Think about it and let me know."

Lena was her last appointment, and Sarah kept her in the office to talk to her a little longer.

This was why she did it. Not because of the procedures, but because she could reassure people. She was blunt and maybe too stubborn. But in her own way, she could be there for her patients. She would be there because no one had really been there for her. Maybe her illness had shaken her confidence in her discipline, her health, her certainty that working harder was the answer to all doubts and doubters. But here, at least for a moment, Lena believed her, and that made Sarah believe in herself. Sarah's patient left pale but with a resolute squareness to her shoulders, and that was something.

The feeling carried Sarah through the evening. She even felt a fizz of energy late that night as she perused her New Experiences

To Do folder. She wasn't going to book a trip to the Galapagos—not now. And singing lessons seemed like an artifact of the past. She was still making notes when her phone buzzed, and she found herself smiling involuntarily—and probably goofily—when she saw Jake's name on the screen.

"Have you recovered from your dad's visit?" she asked.

"I think we're all going to need some time to lick our wounds."

His voice was low and wry, and she felt a swell of—what was it—hope? Heartburn?

"Thank you for both the best and worst date I've ever been on." Jake added.

"Clearly, you haven't gone out much."

"Can you say it wasn't like that for you?"

"It was … unique."

"Are you free tomorrow night? I really want to see you again."

She started unloading her dishwasher. What did it mean that she felt relieved that he had not only forgiven her for getting angry at his dad, but that he also sounded so eager and happy? She felt wanted. And she was excited to see him again, too, which was a frightening thought. She kept her voice casual. "You aren't going to try to seduce me by making my navel into a fruit cup, are you?"

She kind of hoped he would.

"No, that didn't seem to work, so I'm going to seduce you by overwhelming you with science. There's a moon-watching party organized by OMSI. I got a membership to the museum on impulse a few weeks ago."

"For an impulse purchase, that's pretty predictable of you."

"Laugh all you want. They have all of these great programs, like lectures and viewing parties with astronomers and staff, and after-hours wine tastings. Not that I plan to organize all of our outings around the museum—erm, not that I'm assuming that you'll …"

"Another new experience to check off my list," she said lightly. "I'm—I'm looking forward to it."

Another night of Jake. He told her to dress warmly and hung up.

The next night, when he picked her up, there was a picnic basket—price tags still looped around the handles—in the back seat of his car. He drove to the state park, and as they walked down the path, she took his free hand. He gave her his crinkly-eyed smile, and she felt almost giddy.

They stopped and stood for a moment, breathing in the cool, damp air. Clusters of people holding telescopes and binoculars wandered toward a clearing. A few kids ran past, their flashlights cutting through the haze of sunset.

Then Jake began to pull her toward a spot on the far side of the viewing party that he'd decided was perfect. Sarah laughed. It felt … good? Strange to be outdoors in the dark, curiously illicit but also innocent?

She liked holding hands.

They got to the spot, just a little apart from everyone else. She helped Jake spread the blanket and stayed standing to stretch her limbs. As usual, she gave herself a quick check to make sure there were no strange twinges. When she was in med school, she'd never succumbed to second year syndrome. While Petra had especially tended to believe that she had whatever disease she'd been studying, Sarah hadn't bothered worrying. She'd exercised and tried to get enough sleep and stuffed her mouth full of vegetables, and there had been a comfort in that; she'd used it to stop her worries.

Now she self-consciously checked herself. She felt stupid for all the times she'd made fun of Petra. Not that Petra ever returned the teasing. Petra had been the one to insist she go get checked out.

And now Petra was getting married in a month and a half, and Sarah was the disorganized one who'd barely managed to book the yoga retreat for the wedding shower. She didn't know whom she was bringing to the ceremony, even though she'd said she'd bring someone. Apparently, she just didn't know how to celebrate anything anymore, as evidenced by her night on the town with Jake and his father.

As she settled onto the blanket, she considered asking Jake to come to Petra and Ian's shindig with her. She could imagine him in a suit, all sleek vertical lines and warm muscle, holding her close on the dance floor. But she didn't want to put that word *marriage* in his head. He'd just gotten divorced. His ex-wife was re-marrying in a few weeks, and she wasn't sure how kindly he'd look on white dresses and revelry. All of this fuss over cakes and cards was stupid. Except that Petra and Ian's celebration was going to be great because they were her friends and she actually cared about them. And because they would probably be happy together and annoyingly fulfilled in their relationship. So she couldn't even feel cynical about buying them a two-person tent for all the camping trips they were too busy to take.

It *was* on the registry.

"So tonight is supposed to be a perfect night for viewing the moon," Jake said, handing her a bottle of water.

"Perfect night for werewolves."

At his sideways glance, she said, "What? On a clear, moonlit night in the Pacific Northwest, a young woman's fancy turns naturally to *Twilight*."

"Did you read the books? How did you even have time?" He sounded incredulous.

"Yes, during those long stretches of residency when I needed to stay awake."

"Oh, come on. I imagine you studying something, I don't know, educational. Not some vampire series."

"Excuse me, you have a dog named Mulder. Let us not heap scorn on one another's paranormal franchises of choice."

He still looked dubious even as he handed her a container of salad and a packet of dressing and unwrapped a turkey and pesto sandwich for himself.

"You remembered that I don't like sandwiches," she said.

"Yeah. Although, if that's changed, there's turkey with sprouts in the basket. Among other things."

"No, this is"—she almost sighed—"this is perfect."

"Good."

He riffled through the basket a little more, taking out a set of binoculars. "There are telescopes over there if you'd like a better look. But I thought I'd just bring these in case."

She nodded and began to eat.

"So what is it about the books?"

She considered.

"I guess I liked them because they were so much about teenagerhood and about sex and figuring out how to deal with weird bodies. Besides, the small town Washington state setting and a sense of being an outsider in a place that you're technically from—all that hit home."

"So it's not like you secretly long for a powerful man-creature to become obsessed with you and shower you with gifts and also hover over you at night with the threat to tear your throat out with his fangs."

"I think history shows that most man-creatures are pretty capable of tearing people's throats out, fangs or no fangs. So I don't think that part's so much wish fulfillment as it is a reality. Sure some women—or men—enjoy reading about the danger. But some don't. And some stories aren't always what people—no, what *men*—think they are. Young women and teenage girls know that especially."

"I guess that makes sense. The teenage girls I work with speak amongst themselves in a way that's different from the way they talk to other people. It's definitely not the way they usually address me."

"I imagine a few have crushes on you."

"That's happened and we deal with it. But I don't delude myself that they really open up to me. Many of them rightly have trust issues. So they adapt their language when they talk to me."

"If teenage girls speak in code, it's because they're tired of being spoken down to by grown ass men about the subjects that they know far more about. I work with girls, too. They're canny—a lot smarter and more organized than boys at that age. They make mistakes, sure, but they also have more tricks to survive."

"Like you, at that age."

"Like me. Because I had to."

She thought of quiet Lena in her office that day.

Jake didn't say anything, but he scooted closer to her and put an arm around her. And his warmth and the scent of the air, his soap, and the slightly doggy smell lingering on his jacket were immensely comforting. She hadn't even known that she needed that feeling. She'd been so busy focusing on figuring out why she didn't seem to want to work as hard or where her libido had gone, and on being angry or crossing adventures off her list that she'd almost forgotten comfort. Maybe because she'd never had much of it to begin with.

She put down the salad and buried her face in his shoulder, and she felt his other arm move to hold her.

"I like this," she murmured.

She did. She enjoyed the firmness of his body. He shifted to pull her in more securely, and she enjoyed his breath in her hair.

She moved her hand up his stomach and to his chest. She curved her hand around a pec and squeezed.

"Are you taking advantage of this fraught and tender moment to feel me up?" he rumbled.

"Mmm, yes."

"Okay. Good. Carry on."

She sighed again. She almost felt drowsy, but it probably wouldn't be a good idea to fall asleep face-planted in his fleece, on their first official date, before she had even seen the moon through a telescope.

So she pulled herself reluctantly away from his warmth and let the chill wake up her nerves. But instead of being suffused with virtue for taking herself out of his embrace, she was grouchy. Plus, she hadn't felt him up as much as she should have. She rubbed her chilly arms. "Let's get up and look at this moon," she grumbled.

There was a short line for the nearest telescope. While they were waiting, Jake got a call. He looked a little concerned. "It's work. Do you mind if I take this?"

"Go ahead."

A year ago, she would've been the one with the phone pressed to her ear, walking off into the dark. She would've been the one going off to reassure a patient—or even canceling in the middle of an outing in order to rush to the hospital. And she would have missed this—this night sky, the sound of people laughing and talking.

A year ago—and with a different person—she probably would have welcomed the break. Work was so much better, so much easier, than trying to be patient with men.

The blond hipster in front of her turned around. "Sarah."

Sarah looked up into the face of a not-so-recent ex-hookup. Great.

"Oh, hello … Max."

"I thought it was you."

Max moved a little closer. She didn't want to step back, but if she didn't, then she would be practically inhaling the fumes of his hair gel. "That's okay, you can stay where you are," she said, putting her hands out in front of her.

She ardently wished that Jake's caller would be cured of whatever ailed her—and quickly.

Max laughed. "You're such a joker, Sarah."

He moved as if to kiss her on the cheek, and she remembered why she hadn't bothered dating him. She'd tried to talk to him, and that had been a mistake because it was clear that he didn't listen.

"You look good, Sarah."

"Excuse me, are you hitting on my girlfriend?"

From out of nowhere, Jake strode up quickly and got between them, putting his arm around her and effectively pulling Sarah away from Max's lips. At Max's current trajectory, he was about to lean in and make out with Jake's shoulder.

Max, who Sarah remembered as being not particularly quick, stopped and backpedaled.

Bravo.

Jake was not amused, though. She had never seen him look so grim. Even those smiling eyes had flattened to a dark, lethal line.

Max looked confused by this turn of events. "Oh, you two are dating?"

Yep, her memory was correct—Max was definitely not *swift*. It was time to intervene. But Max wasn't done talking. "You're handsome," he said to Jake in a slightly awed voice.

Jake didn't look too impressed with this information, although it certainly was true. In fact, if possible, he looked even better angry. The glower really did something for his eyes and—if she wasn't mistaken—made the tight muscles of his arms stand out in firm relief.

But her lust wasn't really helping the situation—yet. "Yes, he's very gorgeous, and yes we're dating. Max, nice seeing you again, but spin back around so we can make out."

Max turned slowly, his torso moving first, followed by his shoulders, and finally, after a few reluctant blinks, by his head. He seemed confused. By the handsome.

Sarah turned to Jake, ready to make good on her threat, but judging by the stiffness of Jake's posture, he wasn't quite with the program.

"He was going to kiss you," Jake growled.

"He was going for the cheek."

"He was going for your pants."

In front of them, Max's back stiffened a little. He was clearly listening—and longing to turn around. She slid a finger along Jake's tense jaw. He was right. He was no Disney prince right now. All the anger and darkness were bubbling up in him, and Sarah couldn't tamp down the small fizzy thrill that bubbled in her stomach at how hard he seemed.

But this was maybe not where she should be having these feelings.

Jake snorted. "Was that supposed to be a slam by him, calling me gorgeous?"

"He didn't actually use that word—I did. But I don't think it was a putdown. He was sincere."

Jake still frowned. She added, "Plus, you made him completely forget about my pants by arriving on the scene when you did."

Even though it was dark, she could tell that Jake's face hadn't relaxed. "Remember that conversation we just had about going werewolf? Put the fur down, retract the claws, okay? I just told you that wasn't my thing."

"You used to date."

"We went out once or twice."

She added softly. "In the line for a telescope at an OMSI event to see the moon is not the place to exercise aggression. The point is, it was over long ago—if it ever even was—so you don't need to scowl handsomely."

He still looked moody. She pulled very gently on his beard and that made his jaw tense in other interestingly sexy ways. She could imagine nosing her way up the line of his furred jaw to his ear—but he unbent enough to kiss her before it was their turn to observe.

She took her peek first, listening as the guide told her about the way the sun reflected off the moon.

Then it was Jake's turn, and she watched his tense form as he bent over the eyepiece. As he watched, she could see his back relax more and more until he finally straightened up again and thanked the woman in charge.

"What did you think?" she asked.

"Maybe I want a better telescope for my yard," he said.

He was trying to be mild, trying to calm down, because she'd asked him to.

She pulled him away. "It's still bothering you that I used to see that guy. Is this going to be a problem for the rest of the night?"

"If I think about his stupid, smug face, yes." He added, "I never get this angry. About anything."

"Well, if it makes you feel better, I filed him under Stupid Shit I Did in My Twenties along with getting a bob haircut and trying to sing Nancy Sinatra's 'Boots' at karaoke."

"That's such a cliché."

"I know."

"Other than that, I can't imagine you having done any stupid shit in your twenties. Like you said, you were organized and smart."

"Being organized and smart still means you have plenty to figure out. Didn't you do anything stupid in your twenties?"

"I married Ilse."

"Oh. Wow."

She didn't know what to say. His irritation was still there, and it surprised her as much as it did him. Jake had never been unkind about his ex-wife, but now that he had just seen another man at least attempt to kiss the woman he was dating, it had surfaced. She didn't blame him. Sarah almost felt it, too, the sharp twang of confusion and pain—not that he was tied to her through some sort of complicated bond of magic and fate, but because she felt for him. He had always been the kind of person who had been able to put himself in someone else's place. He empathized with people, and now she was feeling for him.

She really hated that woman.

"Let's use the binoculars. It looks like there's some good viewing over there," he said, pointing to a cluster of people.

He didn't want to talk anymore.

That was fine. She wasn't sure she liked where it was going.

CHAPTER ELEVEN

Sarah and Jake stayed late—later than Sarah thought she could stay up nowadays. And despite the fact that Jake bristled whenever Max got within ten feet of them, he managed to relax and talk to the guides and ask questions.

Sarah watched him. He had an easygoing, unobtrusive way of drawing people out. Something about the way he stood, open and yet intimate, the way he listened with his eyes and ears, made the younger people, especially the kids who were out late, want to talk to him. As a result, she and Jake had their own line of people behind them talking about telescopes and phases of the moon.

Sarah put her hand on his thigh as he pulled out of the parking lot, admiring the tense strength of it as he turned around to check for other cars. She stroked it, her fingers moving up in a long, unhurried movement.

He was silent. But after a few minutes, he turned abruptly into a smaller lot and pulled her to his hot mouth in one swift movement.

She felt the scrape of her seatbelt straining at her shoulder and across one sensitive breast. She felt him pulling her, trying to bring her closer, but he was strapped in too, and he didn't seem to want—didn't seem to be able—to stop licking at the inside of her mouth or to take his hand out of her hair.

"Jake," she gasped as his mouth sucked a line down to her neck.

"It's been too long," he growled.

Wet, hot excitement welled deep down between her legs. Her thighs and butt shifted on the seat, straining toward him.

He let go of her suddenly and unsnapped the seat belts that had held them both. "Get in the back," he said, leaning over to open her door.

As he straightened up, he slid his index finger in a line across her chest, right across her nipples, and she gasped unsteadily. Her thighs felt so full and thick with need that she almost couldn't get up and out of the car. The cold outside air seemed almost cruel.

They met each other in the middle of the back seat. He undid the button on her jeans, sliding his hand into them as he pulled her toward him again.

She cried out as his fingers skated across her slippery skin and deep into her. His knee was between her legs, too, and she was caught on him at that one point, almost helpless to do anything but grab at his jacket and his belt and try to take them off him.

He shifted again and banged his head against the top of the car. He cursed, and inside of her, his fingers flexed.

She finally managed to unzip the jacket and push up his t-shirt. His belt came off soon afterward, and she got his pants down part way before the bulge of his erection defeated her trembling fingers.

She could feel his thumb on her clit now, working in the tight space, sometimes connecting just right, sometimes not. She whimpered and tried to move her hips again, to chase that elusive touch.

He let out a frustrated breath and growled in her ear. Then he was pulling his fingers out of her, kissing her, moving his still-damp hand under her t-shirt, the trail of her wetness licking up her spine. He pulled her top off her so quickly that she was momentarily disoriented. Then they were sliding down the seat and he'd stripped off the jacket and her long sleeved t-shirt and unclasped the front opening of her bra, flinging the cups to each side so they dangled like a flimsy vest.

"Tell me what you want," he said.

But it wasn't a query—it was a demand. It was just as well that she couldn't speak, because he was already moving.

Buckles dug into her side, and her thighs were going to cramp while she tried to angle her leg halfway up the seat. It was warm, so warm in the car. The scent of sex and sweat thickened the air, and as he maneuvered himself over her, she finally managed to get her hands under his shirt and down into his jeans for a hard squeeze that made his breath catch—almost choke—before he pushed her down firmly and bent his head to suck on her nipple, then moved down.

"Tell me what you want, Sarah. Do you want me to eat you out with your legs splayed as wide as they'll go in the back seat? Or do you want to get on top of me and fuck my face?"

His question ended on a gasp. Again, he seemed as surprised as she at his words. He was doing this because of *her*, because *she* had transformed him from a quiet man into this desperate, urgent creature.

She drew in an unsteady breath. "I want you. I want you in me."

It was nearly pitch-black in the car with him above her, blocking out any of the light the moon might have given them. She'd forgotten how dark it could get in the countryside. All she had was sound to guide her as she felt her way down his body, but his soft beard and mouth and hands found her again and again with a quick and direct effectiveness. This was not going to be a languorous night.

Let the fucking suit the occasion, she thought before he skimmed his teeth across her ribs and seemed to rear up again.

He was pulling her jeans farther down, pausing to get her shoes and socks off, and then discarding all of the lower body clothing. She heard the crackle of the condom package, the white outline of it pulled over his cock. In the sudden silence she heard herself whisper, "Please, please," thrashing her head back and forth. It was the only movement she could manage now.

She felt the pressure of him before he entered her, the promise that soon he wouldn't be just inside her, but he would be expanding her, making her body and mind stretch beyond what she thought she could be.

She reached her hands up and pulled him down into her, and it was almost as if it pushed the sob out of her lungs.

He thrust hard, pushing her across the seat so that her head banged on the armrest. She cried out. He did it again and reached to pull her leg up over his shoulder. She felt the brush of her foot against the cool window, and he thrust into her again, reaching down to kiss her furiously, his lips and teeth clashing with hers.

And then he was up again, his hand pressing into her clit, and he pulled back with great effort and slammed down again, sliding her across the seat in a hot sear against her back. She twisted desperately under his seeking fingers. His ass flexed again under her palm, and she screamed before he went deep into her again.

The insides of her thighs felt almost raw under the abrasion of his jeans. Her back was slippery on the seat, and she felt stretched wide and cramped at the same time. She had lost command over her limbs. She couldn't even grasp him, couldn't get a handhold on the slippery, tense strength of him under her fingertips as he bucked into her and as his fingers rubbed relentlessly over her wet, hot clit.

One more sharp flick and she was gone, the air streaming out of her lungs as she moaned loud and long, as he thrust into her feverishly, his loud—louder—groans and pants feeding the thick ripples of her orgasm.

A last whimper as he came into her hotly, and they were both still, their breathing harsh in the hot, sweat-and-sex tinged atmosphere of the car.

"Fuck," he said, lowering his weight onto her.

She didn't even complain as the heat of his damp torso pushed her legs to an even more uncomfortable angle. She didn't want him to pull out, so she rubbed her palms along his damp back.

"Stay," she said when he began to move. She was surprised to hear a note of pleading in her voice.

But he stilled. "Aren't you uncomfortable?" he asked, his breath fluting her ear.

She closed her eyes. "I'm fine."

A pause.

"Are we maybe trying to solve some of our problems with sex?"

"That's what grown up people do," she said, her eyes still shut. "Or at least, that's how they should do it."

• • •

He didn't feel like a grown up, Jake thought as the car finally left the park gate.

Frenzied sex in the back seat of a car, almost getting caught by a ranger who shone his flashlight far too long over Sarah's messy hair, over the red line on her cheek where she'd been pressed against the upholstery piping. Luckily, they were both zipped and sitting upright in the front by the time the ranger pulled up, but the lingering scent and their flushed faces made what they'd been doing very clear.

Sarah didn't seem to care, though. She hadn't said much, even to the ranger. She stared somewhere in the distance, an almost-smile pulling at her lips. And she didn't even say much after the ranger ran out of spiel about the dangers of parking in the forest in the dark.

Perversely, that distance, that inward smile, made him want her again, his desire pulling him out of the car and into her house, even as his aching, bruised bones protested.

They went through the same routine of frantic kissing as he walked her backward through her hallway. They pulled off the same clothing, and he smelled her—he smelled himself on her skin, saw the red marks left by his fingers and his car on her hips, saw the scratches inside her thighs, and he pushed his way into her body, eased by the wet from before.

This time, he got to share a glass of water with her before they fell asleep in her bed. Early, early in the morning though, he woke up suddenly, remembering Mulder.

He roused Sarah to tell her he had to go home and take care of his dog. The poor pup was whining by her food dish when he got back. At least she'd used the doggy door to care of her business. He gave her a few treats to appease her, but she was mad at him for having forgotten her. He supposed he deserved it.

CHAPTER TWELVE

Jake hoped that Sarah would be much more forgiving than Mulder. He was ready to call her to make up their date, when Winston's name flashed onscreen.

Jake briefly considered not answering the phone. Word had probably filtered from Jake's father to the Soons—it wasn't as if he and Sarah had planned to keep their relationship a secret—and Jake wondered how careful he should be about Winston's feelings.

Winston—bless his heart—let Jake know right away.

"You're with my sister?" were the first words Jake heard. "After you gave me that bullshit about just checking up on her because she wasn't feeling well? What did she do to you?"

What did she do to you?

Jake tamped down an irrational and somewhat impractical urge to reach through his phone and throttle his old friend. "I don't know, man. Maybe it was those one of those kale juices she gave me."

Winston almost seemed to take him seriously. "What are you talking about? You think she's putting something in the juice? My mom loves that juice. Oh—wait." Winston laughed tentatively. "That's a good one."

Jake felt himself shaking his head. If Winston had been here, he'd probably be slapping him on the back or punching him in the throat—no matter what the answer had been. Maybe later they could have cemented their bond by knocking their foreheads into concrete.

This man was his friend. They'd learned to ride bikes together over a few days on the path behind Jake's house. They'd spilled blood together—mostly as a result of those clumsy attempts at learning to ride, of course. Sarah had tried at the same time as them. But she'd gotten on the pink seat of her tiny bicycle and pedaled away, never falling once.

"So it's just a pity thing, then, huh?" Winston said. "I should have known. You took her out with your dad! You're not really hung up on her? I'm just looking out for you, man."

Jake winced at Winston's hopeful tone. "You know, I can look out for myself, not that I think that's even relevant."

"But people take advantage of your better nature. And you've been married for, like, years. You don't know what it's like out there—what she's like. Who knows what she's been doing all this time?"

"More sorcery and witchcraft? Leading unsuspecting men to their doom?"

"Yes!"

"Listen to yourself, Winston."

"You can't handle someone like my sister. Look, I get it; you've had a crush on her for years. Maybe you even hung out with me because of it—don't interrupt. It's fine. I get it. My hormones were raging all the time, too. But you can't date someone like her, Jake."

"Winston, in the grand scheme of teenaged behavior, Sarah was actually pretty normal."

"But she's my sister."

Jake didn't answer that. He was too angry. It was too much to hope that Winston had given up this stupid idea he'd held in his mind for so long.

"She's too strong. She's selfish, Jake. A total bitch."

"Holy shit, Winston. That's your sister. And she was never selfish."

"Please."

Jake struggled to get words out. The frustration felt thick in his throat. "Is it selfish to not want to do what your family wants you to do? Is it selfish to have opinions, curiosity, independent thought? Even if she weren't your sister, why the fuck would you say something like that about anyone?"

"You don't know her as well as I do. She should have been better than everyone else. And then she just ... left the parents for me to deal with. She doesn't care about the family."

"Like the way they practically abandoned her the only time she seemed to step out of line? I know what happened."

"Jake," Winston said soothingly, "I know Ilse hurt you and you want to get back in the saddle. There are a lot of ladies out there—"

"Why do men keep saying this to me? Why do we keep saying this to each other? We keep talking about saddles and riding along. I'm not a cowboy, and you are a dentist. I'm your friend, Winston. We've known each other since we were kids. I have feelings for your sister and probably always have, but I didn't hang around because of her. I hung around because I liked being friends with you and you were older and I admired you. There. Is that what you need to hear?"

"I don't need your shrink talk, Jake."

"I don't need your bullshit about the way women are and the way men are. And I don't need this stupid bro-business you keep on trying to make us into. We're not bros, and I don't owe that image anything. But I have known Sarah for almost all my life. She isn't some general hazy collection of parts. I know how her eyebrow scrunches when she gets mad. I remember that she's always exactly three minutes early for everything and that she doesn't lie, even when it's polite. And I know when she's hurt and scared. Don't tell me what I can or can't handle. I don't care if I can't handle all of her, Winston, because *I don't need to*. She can handle herself. I'm just glad to know her and be with her."

"You're in love with her." Winston's words were a gasp of outrage. Jake almost wanted to laugh. But Winston's next sentence dampened his urge. "And you think she can love you. She doesn't need you, you know. She's too busy being an independent lady. The minute she's done with you, she'll drop you and she'll break your heart."

Jake thought of every withdrawal, every refusal Sarah had made. He remembered how hard it was to just convince her to go out with him. He thought of how much she mistrusted him. He didn't let Winston hear it, though. "So what if she does? This is none of your business, Winston."

"Everything is everybody's business."

"That doesn't even make sense!"

"No *you* don't make sense."

"Winston, we are not children anymore. You can't just … turn everything around when the conversation isn't going your way."

"Can, too!"

"Can not!"

"Can—"

"I'm hanging up and blocking you if you don't stop this."

"Not if I go first."

In a way, this was probably also pretty typical of their relationship, Jake thought, looking at the "Call ended" screen. He wasn't actually going to block Winston but—

It wasn't their finest hour.

Something about talking to Winston, about dealing with these old memories, with the Soons and his dad, made him feel like a child instead of a thirty-something professional with a divorce behind him and dog under his table. But Sarah didn't make him feel like a child, even though she was caught up in all of that.

Maybe because she didn't treat him like one. Maybe because he didn't act like one when he was around her.

She'd warned him that their families would snarl any happiness—he knew their shared past would complicate things.

Of course, with her flawless timing, Sarah chose to come to his door right then. Mulder barked excitedly as Sarah let herself in and crouched down to let the dog lick her face. Mulder clearly didn't hold Sarah responsible.

She hesitated a bit when she saw him—or maybe that was his imagination. She had some grocery bags slung over her shoulder, and her hair was wet. He still hadn't showered. He wondered if he smelled.

He probably smelled like her.

She came up to him and put her hands on his chest and kissed him, and that felt very good. "You look upset," she said.

"It's nothing. I'm sorry I had to leave last night, but I'm glad you're here. I was—I was just about to call you."

She quirked her brows at him. To prevent further conversation, he lifted her firefighter style. "What has gotten into you?"

"Just doing my job, saving you from the flames, miss," he said. "Uh—"

"I'm told I like to rescue people."

She was a pleasant weight in his arms, and it was fun to haul her around, especially when she seemed to cooperate. *Hah, who's handling her just fine?*

"What am I being rescued from?" she asked as he tromped smartly to the bedroom door and kicked it open.

"Ravening beasts," he said, rolling her onto the bed.

Mulder's claws scrabbled on the hardwood as she ran to catch up with them, but Jake was too quick. He shut the door. The dog whined and whined. At this rate, she probably wouldn't forgive him until dinnertime.

CHAPTER THIRTEEN

Saturday morning: first watercolor class.

Sarah frowned as an orchid she was trying to paint blobbed and ran until it resembled a large ham.

She was used to doing things well. She was not doing this well. She tried to blot it with her fingertip. What she really wanted to do was to rub it all out and start over.

She'd spent much of the week with Jake, and in the course of those days, she'd decided that she was going to ask him to Petra's wedding.

Unaccountably, she felt nervous.

She had been sure of herself last night when they'd had more plans to see each other, but the school had called just as he'd pulled into her driveway—she could hear a man's distraught voice over the cellphone—so she'd kept Mulder and he'd gone off. And she'd fallen asleep on the couch with the dog before his text came.

Was that their life? Had they ... settled? That made her nervous, too. Was he just replacing his married routine with his girlfriend routine? Because they already knew each other in a lot of ways, this relationship was easier than other ones she'd been in. She didn't have to explain her parents' obsession with cleanliness and food, her upbringing, her past. He already knew about Winston and her entire childhood.

But so much of the relationship was new, too. She hadn't known him as a particularly artistic person, but he left little doodles around her house and his. An envelope in the recycling bin had a diagram of Orion. A grocery list on the refrigerator yielded two tiny muscled superheroes punching each other with *Blam! Pow!* blazoned across the top. And once, when she was looking for something to clean a spill, she found a paper napkin with a sketch of a woman stretching. The woman had no features, but Sarah was pretty sure it was her. She smoothed it out and, like the sentimental fool she was, filed it.

She frowned at her own painting again before looking at the clock. She'd never had to take care of a dog on her own before, so she was worried about what might greet her when she got back to the house.

Jake had gone back to his own place to crash before heading to the school. So she had walked and fed Mulder that morning, and she'd enjoyed it. And it made sense, because if he'd wanted to spend the night—if she wanted him to spend the night—then of course he had to bring his dog.

So everything was fine and logical—she liked fine and logical.

But an irrational part of herself wanted reassurance. She'd always been able to rely on herself and external achievements for it, but no one was going to award her a medal for dog-keeping.

The instructor walked by her easel. "Relax your shoulders, ease your grip. Pressing too hard only makes the ink blot."

"I will master relaxing, dammit," she muttered to herself.

She rolled her neck and focused on the page again.

She didn't notice anything amiss when she got home. She'd had a text from Jake saying that he'd come by. He'd also said something about bringing her a bouquet of kale, and even though it was exceptionally cheesy, it made her smile.

She didn't notice at first that Mulder hadn't run to the door. She didn't notice that the house was quiet, because she was used to it being silent.

Not so quiet. As she unloaded groceries, she became aware of a pained panting coming from under the table.

Mulder did not look happy.

She was glassy-eyed and miserable. And she kept pawing weakly at her mouth and drooling—a lot. Mulder was not a drooler.

Sarah pulled a chair out and crawled under the table to give the dog's flanks a reassuring pat. The pup whimpered softly.

Sarah grabbed her phone from her pocket, but as she tried to decide what to do, she heard the door, accompanied by footsteps. "We're in here," she called. "Something's wrong with Mulder. I'm trying to figure out where the nearest vet is."

In a moment, he was under the table with them. Mulder whined when she saw him. Sarah felt guilty and terrible, but now was not the time for it.

"What did she eat?" Jake asked, examining her mouth. "Has she thrown up?"

"I don't know. Maybe. Something's wrong, though. I think you need to take her to the vet right now."

They were both supposed to be the kind of people who were calm in a crisis—she was a doctor and he was a social worker for God's sake. But she could hear the edge of unease in both of their voices.

Enough.

She took a deep breath. "You take her to the animal hospital"— she showed him her phone with the map pulled up—"and I'll stay here and try to find out what she might have gotten into."

He nodded and raced out the door.

• • •

Of course his ex-wife chose this moment to call him. "Sarah, I'm here," he said, not bothering to look at his screen.

A pause. "It's Ilse."

There was a trill indicating a message had come in. Jake sighed. "I can't talk right now. My dog is sick and I'm expecting—"

"Your dog?"

"Ilse, this is a bad time."

He hung up and checked the picture. Sarah had sent a photo of a plant with heart-shaped leaves. And she herself arrived minutes later with the pot.

It took a while, but in the end, Mulder was fine. She'd nibbled a philodendron. A look of annoyance and self-recrimination had flashed across Sarah's face over the fact that she hadn't remembered the name of a common plant. Jake could also tell that she was miserable that Mulder had gotten sick by eating it. And maybe he was sad that all those things had happened, too, but Mulder was fine. It had been an accident. And Sarah was too hard on herself.

Jake wanted to tell Sarah that he was lucky to have her, that he was glad she was around with her cool head. Not that he hadn't handled crises before—he worked with people and kids and their fears and hang-ups all the time—but it was different when he wasn't the only one who could be relied on. She could do some of the thinking and take action. She'd been worried, but that had only made her quick and decisive, and that made him love her even more. Not that he could tell her that right now. It was too soon. Everything he felt was too soon.

So he just said she shouldn't blame herself about Mulder.

But that sounded like such an inadequate thing to tell her— saying that she shouldn't blame herself was almost a way of saying that she should—and it sure as hell wasn't satisfying to him to not unload more of his feelings on her.

Besides, with the specter of Ilse's phone call hanging over him, he needed some time to sort out his head.

"My ex-wife called," Jake told Sarah later. "She ended up leaving a message. To invite me to her wedding."

They were back at his house, sitting on the couch, staring at Mulder while she slept.

Sarah absorbed this news. "Are you actually thinking of going?"

"No."

"Why do you think she invited you?"

That was a good question.

Ilse hadn't been hesitant to dump out all her feelings and questions in the voicemail she'd left. When had he gotten a dog? Was Sarah his girlfriend? He wanted to ask her if she'd thought his life would come to a standstill after their divorce. But of course, the message ended before he could snarl at it.

"Maybe she wants to apologize to me—again. She's very into forgiveness."

"Do you forgive her?"

"Mostly. But inviting me to her wedding is a shitty way of saying sorry—I don't care how good the dancing or food is afterward or if it's open bar. Not that I think there will be any of that."

Sarah frowned.

"I was trying to make a joke," he added. "It's not that I forgive or don't forgive. I just don't want to be there, and I especially don't want to be there for some sort of magnanimous show."

Come to think of it, he did sound bitter—but he wasn't angry about the dissolution of his marriage anymore. He was more annoyed that Ilse was making him deal with her business when he was more than ready to let go. Wasn't that resolution—not letting it get to you anymore? What was forgiveness, anyway? It was pretty annoying if he—the wronged *but no longer angry*—didn't get to pick the terms under which he did it.

The more he thought about it, the more forgiveness sounded like total and complete bullshit. The reverend would be horrified.

"When is it?" Sarah asked, interrupting his thoughts.

"A couple of weeks. The weekend of the fifteenth."

"That's when Petra and Ian are getting married." She paused a beat. "You probably wouldn't want to go to a wedding that weekend, then."

"Why not? Because you think I should stay home and chew on a philodendron while my current girlfriend and my ex-wife dance the night away?"

He knew the words were a mistake when they came out of his mouth.

"Don't say that."

"I'll go with you. It'll be good."

She frowned.

"I'm not going to replace your friends in my mind with Ilse and try to stop the ceremony in a fit of delusion, if that's what you're worried about."

"You're cranky. And maybe even a little mean. You're never mean."

But she was trying to change the subject. And maybe he was going to let her.

"I've earned it today. I was up all night dealing with some freaked out kids and parents. My dog tried to poison herself. And I've been asked to buy a soup tureen and fill it with the warm broth of forgiveness for my ex-wife as a wedding gift."

Sarah nodded. But she didn't laugh like he'd expected—like he'd hoped—she would. "I don't think you have to buy her a present, according to the etiquette books."

"I know. It was a joke. A bad one, apparently."

"Maybe I should go. Mulder's okay."

"Stay."

"I don't know, Jake. I don't know how I feel. I don't know how *you* feel."

"Isn't it good that I can surprise you? Isn't this what you wanted—for me to be a little selfish? A little different from who I am?"

He asked it lightly. But again, she avoided his eyes.

"No, that's not quite it."

She got up and touched Mulder gently, almost tentatively. Then crossed over to the hallway and put on her shoes. That was when he knew that she really wasn't going to stay.

She turned to him and said, "I don't want you to change for the sake of changing."

Then she kissed him, and left.

CHAPTER FOURTEEN

Sarah started following up with phone calls over the next couple of days. She cleared up a coding problem with a billing company and reorganized the files on her phone. Of course, she wasn't quite up to seeing obstetric patients yet, so she hadn't given Joanie the clearance to book them. But for the first time in months, she felt like she was getting things done. She'd even called the yoga studio to book Petra's non-shower/non-bachelorette non-party.

But although she felt energized in her work this week, and although she had spent some time with Jake this week, she felt herself withdrawing.

She told herself it was because she was taking it slow, but this was the way with her, wasn't it? She was interested in someone. It was exciting and new. Then she'd throw herself into her work again. And pretty soon, they were through.

Except she didn't want to be through with Jake. It was new, yes, and yet it was also deeply comforting in a way she didn't quite understand. She knew him—she'd known him since childhood. But she also kept revising her opinion of him, revealing facets. He kept having new feelings she didn't think he had; he kept kissing her in ways she'd never been kissed, showing her new depths. And now her old memories of him were overlaid with new feelings—and that, in turn, subtly shaded and altered some memories of herself.

That was almost a gift.

A gift that she was afraid of—which was why she was in the office stacking books on her tidy desk.

"Still here?" Petra asked, rapping on the door.

"Don't you have fits to throw about escort cards and what color schemes you're going to use?"

Petra leaned in the doorway. "No, Ian's the one who's having fits. If you could call them fits. He's getting nitpicky and overly focused as the date nears. And he's keeping part of it a surprise for me, so he'll hum instead of complaining. I'm starting to hate that humming."

She peered at Sarah's desk. "Is that a pile of books on transcendental meditation?"

"I need to return them to the library."

"Are they any good?"

"I don't know. I forgot how small the print is in paper books. I had such a hard time reading them that let's just say my mood got decidedly unmeditative. Maybe Ian could use them."

"I wish he would."

"You'd think he'd be used to this kind of pressure, running two restaurants."

"When he worries, he works."

"I know that feeling. Except I don't worry. I just work."

"Right. Is that why you're still here then?"

"Nosy Petra." Sarah paused. "I don't know what I'm doing," she confessed. "For a long time, my life seemed laid out well in front of me. I did all the good, right things, and I still got sick. And now Jake wants more; I can tell. And I want more with him—but not while I'm like this and in this strange place."

"You don't have to have it all figured out in order to move forward."

"But I do. I—"

A phone call interrupted them. It was her mother. She told Petra, and her friend looked even more curious. Fai Soon never contacted her daughter at work. "Twice in the space of one month," Sarah muttered as she picked up.

Mrs. Soon didn't waste any time. "We've decided to come for a visit. In a week and a half."

Sarah couldn't say anything for a minute. Seeing the look on her face, Petra waved frantically in alarm.

"San-san, are you there?" her mother prompted.

"You can't come. Not in a week and a half." *Not ever.* "My friend is getting married and I'm involved with the wedding and I won't be able to do anything with you."

"You aren't part of the wedding party, are you?"

"Well, no. But—"

"You don't want us to go there?"

She didn't want them anywhere near her. But they never took vacation—they only took Sundays off for church—because they believed in work. And they'd certainly never gone to Portland, because they never stopped being disappointed in her. They worked hard at that, too. It took a lot of discipline to be Ma and Pa Soon. She'd gotten her own from them.

"You're right. I don't want you to visit."

It seemed a terrible thing to admit to her mother, to say it right out loud: if she didn't care, she wouldn't have had trouble saying it. But she did. Despite all the distance, all the neglect from both sides, she still cared what her parents thought.

But her bluntness didn't seem to faze her mother. It was that unflappability that got things done. "You have always been contrary. But we've already arranged the schedule, so we're coming. Marian will be in charge of the store, and our neighbor Jenny will come in and water the plants."

"Water the plants! How long are you planning on staying?"

"At least a week. We'll bring supplies."

Sarah could not help it. She squeaked. "You're staying with me?"

"Of course we are."

"But—"

"I'll call you when we arrive."

"I—"

Her mother had hung up.

"You know, I've never seen you panic before," Petra said after another minute had passed.

"My parents have never visited me, and now they're staying for a week and she won't take no for an answer."

"She sounds a lot like you," Petra murmured.

"She *is* a lot like me. This is a disaster."

"If the two of you are in one place, what happens? A black hole?"

"We lived together for the first seventeen and a half years of my life. The universe stayed intact."

"But you hadn't become you."

"I have always been this way."

"People like you don't spring fully formed from the J. Crew catalog."

"My parents are here to save Jake from my evil influence. And I don't even know if I want him in my clawed devil fingers. It's more like he's choosing to roll around in my palm."

"Dirty."

"Will you shut up? I have to think. I have to organize. I have to *clean*."

"Your house is immaculate."

"*Not. Immaculate. Enough.*"

"Do you really think this is about Jake and you?"

"Of course it is. They haven't taken a trip in … as long as I can remember. They worked in that hardware store six days a week from 7:00 a.m. till 8:00 p.m. for thirty-five years straight. Both of them—and both of us kids spent hours there, too. And now suddenly they decide to take a whole week of vacation? Just when I start dating the reverend's son?"

"Do you think they're for or against it?"

"I don't know. Both options are terrible. If they're for it, they'll jump straight from dating to marriage and retirement plans and grandchildren. If they're against it, then I worry for Jake. I'm used to dealing with them, but they know him well enough to go directly at him."

"And you think he'll give up like that?"

"Not easily. He's not a pushover, and nothing to do with my parents is ever restful. It's too much conflict."

She was the one who didn't want a fight for a change. She pressed her lips together. Since when had she become such a coward?

"So are they really staying with you?"

"Yes."

"I didn't hear you offer."

"I didn't. It's understood."

"Well, *I* don't understand. Why can't they go to a hotel? Surely you'll all be less miserable."

"It's hard to explain. "

"You don't usually have a hard time telling people your opinions."

"Parents are a difficult blind spot, though. And then there's the fact that sometimes they don't care about your opinions. And mine don't give a shit about my boundaries. Which is maybe the real reason why I'm not close to them. It's so ingrained—and I see it and it frustrates me. But I can't stop it. So you're right. I didn't spring fully formed from the J. Crew catalog. I had a lot of upbringing. It's like the way I sort of have kept in contact with them, even though we're mostly estranged. I can't take that final step and sever relations with my parents. And so I go along with their rare and occasional demands."

"Are you going to bring your mom to the office?"

"I'd rather not. She'll probably make an appearance anyway."

Petra nodded. "I kinda want to meet her. Should I invite them to the wedding?"

"God, no. You sound a little too much like you're enjoying this. Aren't you the teensiest bit supportive? Or sorry for me?"

"I'm a complicated woman. I'm a little of all of those things."

"Thanks, Pete. You're a pal."

"I am. And this isn't the worst thing you've been through—not by a long shot."

That was true enough.

"Anyway," Petra continued, "did you ever consider the possibility that your parents might have changed?"

"Changed. What does that even mean?"

Petra started out the door. "Go home. Start cleaning. I know that's what you want to do."

CHAPTER FIFTEEN

Jake had been warned, but he hadn't expected to see Mr. Soon bent over the stones in Sarah's yard, scrubbing them with a strong brush.

"Outdoors is filthy," Mr. Soon grunted when he straightened and saw Jake.

"It does tend to get that way. Uh, how was your trip?" Jake asked.

"Long."

Sarah's tables and chairs were crammed onto the porch, along with a lamp and a rug.

Mr. Soon went back to scrubbing.

Jake was glad he hadn't brought Mulder along. She'd probably be in a bucket full of suds before her paws landed on the ground. He walked through the open door. The living room furniture was covered in tarps. In the kitchen, Mrs. Soon was on a ladder, cleaning the top of the fridge.

"Do you know why she has so many filing cabinets?" Mrs. Soon asked him by way of greeting.

Sarah *did* have a lot of filing cabinets.

Jake weighed his words. "She likes to be organized?"

Mrs. Soon grunted.

"I can help you with uh, that thing you're doing, if you want," Jake offered.

She waved him off.

He peered out the door and saw Sarah standing in the backyard staring at the fence.

"Hey," he said.

She turned and gave him a weary smile.

"How are you doing?"

"I feel like peeing in the corners of my house to mark my territory."

"It has nothing to do with you; you know that right? Your parents just have to … clean to feel comfortable. And after they're done, then maybe they'll be ready to talk."

"Talk. Ugh. Maybe that's worse than the cleaning. You're not helping."

Jake thought for a minute. "C'mon," he said. "Let's knock some more off of your to-do list."

He held out his hand. Sarah hesitated, then took it.

They walked back through the kitchen. Mrs. Soon stopped scrubbing and watched them. She even pointed her chin at their clasped hands—subtle wasn't her style—but didn't say anything.

"We're just going out for a little while," Jake said, cheerily.

He pulled Sarah along, but perhaps not surprisingly, Mrs. Soon followed. "Are you coming back for dinner?"

Jake answered. "Yes, we'll be back. Thanks."

Mrs. Soon pursed her lips.

"I think by pulling me away from the sanitizing you just made a formal proclamation that you aren't going to be a nice quiet boy who sits and waits and does anything they want," Sarah told him when she got in the car.

"I was mostly signaling that I was too lazy to help clean."

"She probably thinks we're sneaking off to have sex, Jake."

"She thinks—she suspects—but she's not sure, because it's me. Kind Jake who would never do wicked things with her wicked daughter."

"You find all of this hilarious! I can't believe it: you're devious."

"You love it."

"But she hates it, and she's going to give you an earful. I hope you're ready for that."

"Oh, I'm ready, sweetheart. I was born ready."

He gunned the engine, and she burst into laughter. "I didn't know you could make a Honda Civic sound that ferocious."

He pulled out of the driveway. "If you think that's hot, wait till you see what I can do with my juicer."

• • •

"That wasn't on the original list," Sarah murmured a little later.

Jake had good intentions. He had a plan—not a great one—to drive out to the beach, but Sarah couldn't keep her hands to herself once she got in the car. And because he was such a responsible citizen, they pulled into Jake's drive. She unzipped him even before the garage door closed.

Parking. Again. They were really feeling like teenagers.

By the time they stumbled into the house, Sarah's dress was shoved up and her underwear pulled down. He stumbled through the hall as he watched her lithe waist and her little round butt flex and tense as he followed her in.

They made it to his foyer before she turned and tugged on his t-shirt. He still had his keys in his hand, so he put them down carefully on the table and pushed her back until her ass bumped against it. She reached down into his jeans. He grabbed her wandering hand out before she could get him in more trouble, but she rolled her hips, bumping against the edge of the table. A breath hissed between his teeth.

He needed to get a grip on himself—on something. He put his arms down on either side of her, and she bumped him again, that single provocative contact of her hips making him tighten to the point of pain. He clenched the edge of the table, his knuckles white—one hand, and then the other.

Her body stretched up slow. "I think you're a bad influence," she said, her voice close to his ear.

She put that hand up again and let it hover in the small space between them. They were both watching it carefully. Her finger arrived at his pec, and he let out a grunt as if she'd hit him with a blow to the gut.

"You didn't stop to chat with my parents. You just came in and swept me away. And they let you get away with it because you fooled everyone. Everyone thinks you're good."

"I *am* good."

He pulled her dress up and off in one swift movement. He unsnapped her bra ruthlessly in the next, balled up the pretty lace, and tossed it over his shoulder. She shivered, and he blew a breath over her. He loved her breasts. He loved the shallow dip that divided her ribcage so warm and soft, the nap of that skin, the delicate, flared architecture of waist and hip, the alluring shadow of dark hair between her legs. His fingernail traced every line gently, so gently that when he took it away, he pulled a gasp out of her. She narrowed her eyes at him. "If you're so good, why did you make me deviate … from my list?"

He grinned. In a sudden movement, he forced his legs between her thighs so that they were now wedged wide to him. He wasn't quite there, at the center of her, where he knew she wanted him to be. She tried to squeeze herself together and rub herself against him, but she was perched on the edge of a spindly table. She was off-balance, and he liked that.

He leaned down deep and lapped her collarbone, and she arched so far back that her head hit the wall. She grabbed his back for balance and tried to haul herself against him, and finally he let his arms come around her and pressed himself right there, right where she wanted and ached.

She gave a little scream of frustration, and he twitched with suppressed laughter—and some pain.

"Damn you," she said, before biting right into his shoulder.

That was too much for him. His hips thrust, and the poor yard-sale table gave a dangerous creak. The keys crashed to the floor. In a panic she wound her legs around him.

She was nose to nose with him now, and he felt an unkind grin stretching at his features. "Danger follows me everywhere."

"You—"

But she kissed him. While their mouths moved together, he pulled her off the rickety table. He backed her against the cold wall, and she gave a startled yelp. He took advantage of her movement to bring his mouth to her breast, then down, down further.

He forced himself to calm down. To slow. Between lazy licks under her breast, he looked up and said, "You know, I think I'm going to start my own list." His voice was impressively steady. Good. "Because," he added, "I've never eaten anyone out against a wall before."

She panted. "You don't seem to need any instruction from me anymore."

He took a deep breath. "I'm learning. But we'll see."

He eased her thighs apart, rubbing his palms against their faint dampness. He wanted to just nuzzle her, to rub his cheeks against the tender inner skin and absorb the sharp scent of her into his pores. But she was already trembling, trying to grip the walls, and she wouldn't last long. So he pushed his lips against her and licked. She shuddered and sank down slowly. He gripped her thighs with two hands to steady her and sucked and licked again.

She sank lower and so did he.

It was quick after that. Her thighs flinched—just the quickest movement of her skin. He ran his thumbs along the taut grooves of her legs, up that gorgeous swell of her ass as he licked steadily, right there in that delicate spot, the precise point that made her cry out.

They were naked in the front hall on the floor now, her back straight against the wall, her legs clamped over his shoulders. She still wearing one shoe, and it thumped wildly against his back as he pulled and sucked. Then she screamed and he felt her pulse around him, and she gripped him tight between her legs.

The house creaked with its old house noises. But otherwise, it was quiet. Illicit.

He let go of her briefly to scramble for a condom. As he rolled it on, she reached her hand out, traced a line around his pectoral, and dotted his nipple gently, like a kid drawing dirty pictures in class. She was admiring him, and it hurt so damn much to be admired by someone as wonderful as she.

"Can you stand?"

"I can try. I've never done this against a wall either. I'm going to write it on my list to cross it off."

"Don't overexcite yourself," he growled.

He pulled her up again. Then in one surge, he was all over her hot skin, nipping at her neck as he rocked against her, or was she working herself on him, up and down, with all the hard and soft pieces of their bodies providing friction and heat. He pushed into her until it felt like he couldn't go deep enough, and then turned her so that she faced the other way and he bent her down and dug his fingers into her hips.

She slapped her hands on the wall and whimpered. It was such a terrible support. He clamped an arm around her waist and slipped his other hand down between her legs, seeking her clit clumsily and blindly because she was going to have to come again. She had to.

It was enough. She cried out again, arching up, higher and higher until she was almost on the tips of her toes. The blood was surging through him, making him lightheaded, almost incandescent with pleasure and panic. They were going to crash, and he wasn't going to be able to save her. Her head flew backward almost into his shoulder, and her mouth opened on a silent cry. He groaned. That was all it took. His arms were around her, but he had let go.

• • •

After cleaning themselves up, they stumbled into bed for an afternoon nap. Sarah couldn't sleep. Jake lay on his stomach, his leg latched through hers as if he knew she was going to try to crawl away. His breaths came deep and long and comforting. She wanted to smooth his hair back, but she couldn't lift her arm. They had exhausted each other.

Her thoughts were confused, though, and every time she managed to drift, a tickle of worry had her eyes fluttering open. She was glad that he'd taken her away. Yes, she could deal with her parents—it hadn't been all bad—but sometimes it was so nice not to have to always be the one who said something. Sometimes it was good just to have someone who didn't think she was overreacting to two harmless-seeming elderly people.

But she just didn't know what to do with it—what to do with Jake, who was becoming more and more different from the Jake she had known. She was the one who'd told herself she had to change after her cancer scare, but he was the one who was really turning himself inside out—he had taken her words to heart. He was all in.

Was she?

And this afternoon, the way he'd just pulled orgasms out of her, she didn't know what to do with that—a normal person would just enjoy it. And she had at the time—really, really enjoyed it. A lot.

But now she just couldn't leave it alone.

Who was he going to be at the end of this? And was he going to need her at the end of it all? She'd tried so hard to become self-sufficient, and now—she was with him, and that whole strained line that connected her to her family was a web. They were so intertwined already—because they'd grown up together, because they were together now.

At one point, he'd draped his arm over her waist, but she'd wriggled free so that she'd feel less bad about tossing and turning. But she didn't quite want to stop touching him. Even now, she moved her restless foot up and down his calf, feeling the strength, feeling the calm.

For all her bluster about not caring, she had been the one playing along with her parents' visit and letting them do God knows what to her house and psyche. But he had been willing to cut ties in his life. He'd done the hard stuff. He'd gotten the divorce. He'd been plain and direct with his father. He was willing to face up to it.

She admired him, which was a cold and distant word for what she actually felt. She also felt grateful, which seemed like an even scarier, colder word, full of cringing, and yet that wasn't how it was for her either. How she felt was flower petals on her skin and rushing warm lust and this even stronger throb of love somewhere deep in her chest.

He'd been courageous. She wasn't sure she was brave for all her bravado.

For the first time in a long time, she was going to have to take a hard look at what she wanted—not what she thought she wanted or what she was supposed to want, but what she really wanted.

And she was afraid that it was Jake.

She must have twitched, because Jake's arm came over her again, pulling her close. He was warm, and he smelled like a little bit like sweat and a little bit like that manly man's masculine shower gel she'd made fun of him for buying. He was nuzzling her, still mostly dozing, and it made her feel wonderful and miserable at the same time.

But he must have been more awake than she thought, because he said, "Can't sleep?" and rolled her into a firmer position at his side. He acted like he was not going to let go.

CHAPTER SIXTEEN

Jake got Sarah back to the house a little later in the evening than he'd planned. Well, there wasn't much of a plan. He really had started out wanting to take her to do something new and interesting—something she could cross off that list. Maybe he should feel accomplished that they had done something new, considering exactly how many new things she'd tried (once) over the last months.

Instead, they showered and tried not to look too blissful, lest the gods and/or Sarah's parents rain judgment upon them. They brought Mulder back with them and put her in the backyard before heading into the house. The furniture was gone from the porch—and no doubt assembled in a new arrangement inside the house—and the smell of cooking permeated the air.

"You're late," Mrs. Soon observed as they breezed in.

"We didn't settle on a time," Sarah singsonged.

Nonetheless, Jake felt her grip tighten on his arm.

Mrs. Soon watched them but didn't say much. Her silence sobered him. He'd known Mrs. Soon—Fai Soon—all his life, which only increased his wariness.

They ate efficiently—making their way through piles of greens in relative silence. Jake was going to help Sarah with the dishes when Mrs. Soon held him back.

She led him to the front porch and fixed him with her eye. "Are you planning to marry her?"

Well, that cleared up which tack Mrs. Soon was planning to take. The question was—what did he want? "It's early. I think we both need to take our time. We've only been seeing each other for—"

"You've known her for more than thirty years. It is not early. Are you only with her because you're lonely after your divorce? You think you can have a party with her?"

"A party. That's what you think. No. I am with her because I want to be with her."

"You're using her."

"If you think that, then you don't know me. And clearly, you don't know your daughter well at all."

She drew back. It seemed he had scored a direct hit. But he felt no pleasure in it. He knew he was lying on some level. He did want to be with Sarah—wake up to her in the mornings and walk the dog with her. He might even want to marry her. But he didn't want to think about that right now. Sarah wasn't ready for him. If he asked now, she'd say no and she would cut him right off. Right now, the knowledge that she wasn't there yet was only a dull ache. But he couldn't tell her mother that.

"Even your father is dating again. A girl."

Jake wasn't aware of all the nuances at play, but the way Mrs. Soon said "dating" and "girl," drawing out the last consonants, seemed to indicate that she didn't approve—although whether it was of dating or this particular girl—woman, *thirty-something professional physician*, he corrected himself—he didn't know. "Why should it matter that my dad is dating?"

"Well, what would your mother have said?" she murmured to herself.

He considered being flip. He thought about pointing out his father wouldn't have been with the girl if his mother were there. But Mrs. Soon looked perplexed and thoughtful.

They had been best friends, his mother and Mrs. Soon. He remembered his mother had been glad to have someone to talk to, even though his mom was from Taiwan and Fai Soon was from China. In their birthplaces, it might have made a difference, but together in the United States, they could form a bond. Not that either woman had been shy or retiring. Mrs. Soon talked with people all day at the hardware store, advising them on the best nails to hang drywall and barking on the phone to see if the orders of barbed wire had come in. His mother was a paralegal and had taken an interest in town politics—he seemed to remember a lot of talk between the two about streetlight design.

The illumination of Main Street was as good a thing to cement a friendship as any, he supposed.

"Your dad is a minister. I suppose he knows what he's doing," she said. "But it is strange to think of your father with someone other than your mother."

"For me, too."

"How do I know you won't be like that with Sarah? That you'll forget her if—if something happens to her?"

Fury simmered in Jake's chest. "So what is it? Am I not good enough for your daughter, or am I too good for her? Make up your mind."

She didn't answer. He almost laughed—almost—at the delicate calculations she was trying to make.

"I don't want her to be hurt."

"*Now* you're protecting her?"

She drew back. Apparently, he could surprise her. But she recovered quickly. "You need to be more respectful."

It was on the tip of his tongue to apologize—it was conditioning. But anger was boiling in his chest, and he wouldn't mean it. Sarah wouldn't have done it. "And here I thought you were going to tell me that I'm too good for her, the way Winston does."

"No."

"You say that, but you still don't know how good she is. You don't appreciate the value of her."

"Sarah has not had it easy, but she never made it easy on herself. It could have been different if she did not fight me all the time."

"So you want her to just roll over and have no opinions and not decide what she wants to do."

She was indignant. "Of course that's what I want for her. Having opinions is terrible. It makes you unhappy with everything in the world."

"You have a lot of opinions."

"I'm old. I'm allowed. I am hard on her because the world is hard and she needs to learn how to deal with it. What do you know about difficult anyway? Softhearted boy. Your mother was my good friend, but she and your father were too easy on you. Which is why you help people *as a job*."

Definitely disdain.

Well, he was getting tired of it from this family. First Winston, now her. "Yes, Mrs. Soon, every day I see how hard the world is and, as you say, I help people for a living. You don't have to tell me how difficult life can be, because I know something about what it's like, and I am tired of people like you, Mrs. Soon. So fucking tired. You weren't the outside world for Sarah. You didn't need to be hard. But you were. And because you decided you needed to make existence even worse for your kids, you can step back and stop pretending that Sarah needs you, because you never gave her anything. So stop cleaning her house, because it's not yours. You weren't even here when she was sick."

Mrs. Soon recoiled again. "She said she wasn't that sick. She said she didn't want us."

"I don't blame her. When have you ever been here for her? And now, you wait until she's recovered, and then you come out here and tell her what to do? I don't even know what to say to you."

He didn't even bother to look at her face. He was far too angry, and he didn't want to spend any more time on the porch with her. He walked down the steps and around into the backyard. In a minute, he heard the door open, and Sarah stepped out.

She put her hand on his arm briefly, and then it was gone. "I heard everything."

He forced himself to sound light. "Even the sexy growling at the end?"

"You know how to make an eavesdropper pay attention, that's for sure."

He was silent. He wasn't sure how she'd taken his words with her mom. She hadn't wanted to be defended—he'd known that. He'd known that even as he berated her mother.

Jesus. He'd berated Mrs. Soon.

He sneaked a glance at Sarah, but she was turned away from him.

He ventured, "I think I may have even won the argument."

"She plays the long game."

"I know. Your mom is kind of a ruthless asshole. A well-meaning, completely horribly misguided, and unrepentant asshole."

Sarah laughed, but it sounded so sad that his heart made a long, queasy flip. "Not always well meaning," she said.

He rubbed his face. "It was less satisfying telling her off than I thought it would be. I usually keep myself in check. But I'm angry with her, and I almost feel like rolling around in my anger and going inside and rubbing it all over the furniture. I mean, how have you lived with her for twenty-four hours? How is it even possible?"

"See? Long game. My mom might break you yet."

Her voice was light, but she still wasn't looking at him.

"She may have winded me, but I got in a few good ones, too."

"More than a few."

Another pause.

She turned very deliberately to him. "You didn't have to tell her any of that, you know."

She said this almost wistfully, and his heart gave one loud painful thump.

"But—I hear a but in there."

"But I also don't need you to do this."

"Don't need or don't want? Tell me this, Sarah, why am I always trying to draw us nearer and why are you always moving away? Your mom is worried that I won't care for you, that I won't be here. But it always seems like the opposite to me. You don't want to come close."

"I want to. I want to so much."

"There's that but again."

A pause. "This stuff is more complicated. At a certain point, I have to fight these fights myself. You think you know me and my life—"

"I am trying, but you are stopping me. I am here asking you to let me help you. But you don't trust me to stick around to help you."

She said nothing.

"That's it, isn't it? You don't trust me to help you."

"You just got out of a marriage."

"That is unfair and not the reason—"

"No. No, you know a lot of things about me. You know some things I don't know. But I don't want to upset the balance that I have with my parents. The relationship I have with them was hard won."

"What relationship? What balance? The one where you are basically polite acquaintances?"

She grimaced. "I wouldn't say that we're polite."

"No, Sarah. Listen to yourself. This isn't about them. Even now you're deflecting. You keep making it about them, and that's what's going wrong. It's about you and me. I can live like this for a while. But at some point, I am going to need more from you, too."

"Don't say that. Don't make more demands on me."

"I have to say it. If I don't, you'll never know how much I care." He pulled her to him and gave her a hard kiss. "Your choice," he said.

And he forced himself to walk away.

CHAPTER SEVENTEEN

Sarah tossed and turned on the creaky mattress in her guest room, went to work, and came back to find that her parents had stopped their cleaning and her tiles had been re-grouted. They ate silently and glumly at the kitchen table, and after doing the dishes, Sarah went and hid in her room.

It was like being a teenager again. Except with better Wi-Fi.

She resolutely did not call Jake. She put him firmly out of her mind with the help of the *Twilight* movies and Words with Friends. One part of her thought that if she were on call, she could be at the hospital delivering babies. Was she ready? Maybe she missed it. Besides, it wasn't as if she was getting much sleep nowadays.

Yet she wanted her return to be flawless. She couldn't accept any help. She couldn't make any mistakes. And until she was perfect, she wouldn't be going back.

But of course, she wasn't honed and ready. Her fight with Jake had proven that. He had asked her to trust him, and her response had been to withdraw. But he was frightening. Jake, who just by existing and being with her brought too many parts of herself together—too many eras—and who made her realize that the walls she used to keep everything apart were thin. What would she do without them?

But what would she do without him? There was no doubt that her mother had been—well, gentler was not the word. But she had seemed more subdued and maybe thoughtful ever since her conversation with Jake. And Sarah was so grateful about this, so eased by it that it scared her even more that she could depend on him.

She wanted to call him. But she didn't.

By 5:00 a.m. she was up and making coffee. Her father padded in in his slippers and sat down. She silently poured him a cup and pushed the stevia syrup at him.

He shook his head. "Gave that up. Too highly refined, too many additives. You aren't up on the research?"

She wanted to bristle, but the best she could manage without caffeine was a wince. "I bought it for you when I heard you were coming."

"Oh, well … " He contemplated the bottle. "Don't want to waste it."

He stirred a judicious amount in and capped it.

Sarah snorted. *Don't want to waste it* was her father's excuse for eating, well, anything. She suddenly missed him, even though he was right there, grimacing at the taste of his first sip.

She sat down and stared at her mug while her father puttered around and made toast. Neither of her parents were able to stay still for long. She hadn't been able to stay still for long, but she'd tried to learn it recently.

Item #4: *Stay still.*

"Jake wasn't around yesterday."

Ugh. First they wanted Jake gone; now they wanted him clinging to her like a baby monkey. Her dad handed her a slice of wheat toast with some kind of sprouted sunflower spread he'd concocted.

"I told him we needed a little break."

"Winston will want to see him."

"Oh great. Winston's coming? When were you going to let me know about that?"

"I asked him for next week. He'll be at"—he wrinkled his nose—"a hotel."

He shook his head.

"I don't have time for another guest. I have my best friend's wedding. And I have to attend the pre-wedding activities."

"So Winston can entertain us while you and Jake are watching your friend get married."

"Winston's not a dog. He can't do tricks—not any good ones, at least. And he's never been to Portland. How would he entertain you?"

"We can take care of Jake's puppy while you two are busy with wedding activities. And we can use a guide book."

Sarah stayed quiet. She didn't know if Jake was coming with her to the wedding, and she was going to have to find out soon.

She was distracted again by her father's next words, though. "Jake was right—about some things he said to your mother. We should all talk as a family."

Jake again.

She swallowed. "You want to *talk*? I can't think of anything I want less."

"Me neither," he said glumly. He took a big slug of coffee. "But your mother wants it to happen. I think she was hoping that it would come about"—he paused to try out the word—"organically."

Sarah almost snorted her coffee.

Her dad good-naturedly thwacked her on the back.

After she stopped coughing, she waved her hand. "Right. Well, I guess if it doesn't work, then Mrs. Fai Soon will bludgeon it into happening."

Her father laughed and rinsed his dishes. "I'm going to make a porch swing and put it up," he said casually.

And he ambled out of the house.

• • •

It wasn't until her mother showed up downstairs when Helen arrived with Petra that Sarah realized another secret horror.

"Going to yoga! On a weekday? Can you afford to take this time off?"

"It's just one day."

"You already don't work that much."

"I work all the time."

"I haven't seen you do one thing."

Helen was chortling quietly.

But Fai Soon had already leaped to another topic. "May I come with you to this yoga class?"

"No! Mom! It's a celebration for my friend. It's not an open class." Sarah turned to Petra. "I'm sorry."

"I am not a pet," her mother said. "You do not have to apologize for the messes I make."

"It would be fine to have another person," Helen interjected cheerfully.

"But it's the bachelorette party and-or wedding shower."

They really needed to settle on a name for this thing.

"You said Pete's mom is going," Fai said.

"Her name is *Petra*—"

"You call her Pete."

"And *Petra's* mom is going because Petra's mom is the goddamn mother of the bride."

"Don't swear, San-san. I am very good at yoga. And I can pay my share."

"Where? How? How are you good at yoga?"

"A young woman opened a studio in town a few years ago. I invited you to come that *one* time you came to visit. There is yoga and Pilates and weight training. I like it. I talked to the lady about getting a teacher's certification. If her business keeps getting better, she said she would think about it. Your dad prefers Pilates," she added. "Your father has champagne taste."

"I actually think it would be fun to have your mom along," Petra said.

"I'm not riding with her," Sarah snapped.

"Do you insist on using the GPS?" Helen asked Fai.

Sarah's mom wrinkled her nose.

"Great!" Helen said, linking arms with Fai. "We can take two cars. Sarah, you drive Pete. I'll go ahead with your mom and get things organized. Mrs. Song, you can give me all the dirt on what Sarah was like as a kid."

Sarah's mom practically skipped upstairs to get her gear, and Helen wisely took herself to her car.

"I'm being a brat," Sarah said.

"You've never cared about it before," Petra said. "Besides, having acted like a brat as an adult with my own difficult mom, I can sympathize. C'mon, this is going to be fun."

It was fun for Petra—she was the bride-to-be after all. It was not quite so for Sarah.

Sarah's mother had not been lying. While the rest of them grunted and groaned through a one-hour session, Mrs. Song was serene and impressively limber. She slid into a shoulder-pressing pose, and Sarah went cross-eyed to keep herself from swearing.

Helen nudged Sarah. "How 'bout them flexy genes?"

"Her being able tuck herself into a tiny crab cake is not genetic, you idiot. It's daily practice. It's work."

"Some component is definitely genetic. I'm bendy, but I'm not shaped like a person who could ever be a crab cake. I do better as a crane or something long and graceful."

"Shut up, Helen."

"I've never seen you sweat this much."

"This is why I avoid doing yoga with you. You're a former ballet dancer *and* you're chatty. Basically, you're every normal yoga practitioner's worst nightmare."

A pause and they dropped into another pose.

"You're not normal, and why would you want to be? Seriously, your mom is inspiring me. How old is she? Sixty-five?"

"Sixty-four. Ugh. I never thought flexible would be a word I could apply to my mother in any way, shape, or form."

"Like you said, it's work."

The teacher finally shushed them.

People could work and change, Sarah thought as they stood around drinking cucumber and coconut coolers. Petra's mother, Lisa, and Sarah's mom were having an animated conversation that dissolved into a few giggles and involved the sloshing of some of the liquid in the glasses. They were even leaning on each other. And Sarah's mom looked a little red—

Belatedly—and maybe a little dizzily—Sarah realized that there was quite a bit of alcohol in the drinks.

She turned to Helen—too quickly. "Oh my god, did you spike these?"

Petra sidled up, bright-eyed. "I did!"

She held up a flask.

"Jesus Christ, Petra. What were you thinking? My *mom* is drinking them. We don't metabolize alcohol well. You know that."

"I thought they would taste good. There's hardly any. Besides, you'll have time to sleep it off during massages."

"Hardly any is a lot for me. And her. I don't think I've ever even seen my mom drink. I have to go save her."

She lurched toward the mothers, with Petra and Helen following.

Lisa Lale was asking Fai about growing goji plants. Of course. Lisa said, "My new boyfriend is an oncologist, and he says that goji berries and black sesame seeds are worth adding to your diet.

Of course, they're both things that get stuck in your teeth, but luckily I started carrying around these little floss picks."

Petra's mom looked like she was ready to whip out her personal dental hygiene equipment, when Petra interrupted her. "Wait, Mom, what is this about a new boyfriend?"

Lisa was suddenly quiet.

"You broke up with Jim Morrison?"

"Your boyfriend is named Jim Morrison?" Fai asked.

Petra's mom flushed. "Old boyfriend. *Former* boyfriend."

"When did this happen? You said you were bringing Jim. I have escort cards printed up with his name on them," Petra said.

Her face was now as flushed as Sarah's.

"I said I was bringing *James*," Lisa said.

Fai said, "You broke up with a Jim and you're dating a James?"

Lisa nodded.

"What's his last name?"

There was a pause.

"It's, uh, Taylor."

There was another silence.

Petra said, at last, "Okay, I am aware that I'm repeating myself—"

"It's been a whirlwind," Lisa said.

"You broke up with Jim Morrison."

"Yes."

"And your current boyfriend is named—"

"Yes."

Petra whipped out her phone. From another corner of the room, Ellie, Petra's sister chortled, "I guess you could say Mom's going for the whole Jimmy buffet."

Beside her, Sarah felt Helen shaking with suppressed laughter as Ellie exclaimed, "What? You think I'm going to pass up the opportunity to make that joke?"

"You've already made it three times," Lisa snapped.

"We're going to have to change the place cards, too," Petra said into the phone. More loudly, "Mom, why didn't you say anything? Did you think I wasn't going to notice you traded one Jim for another? Did you think *he* wasn't going to notice?"

"You should respect your mother," Fai said sharply, looking at both of Lisa's daughters.

Instantly, they all quieted and stood up a little straighter. Sarah found herself almost envying Fai Soon's ability to shape up a room full of tipsy women. Well, almost everyone. Helen was still on the verge of bursting into giggles.

Meanwhile, Fai had glided to the middle of the floor, glowing softly and redly under the gorgeous natural light of the yoga center's solarium. Sarah could almost admire her mother but—

"I'd like to make a speech," Fai said.

Correction, she admired her mother except when her mother was an embarrassing jerk. But Petra, Helen, Lisa, and Petra's sister and sister-in-law stamped and whistled—probably in relief—and effectively drowned out Sarah's loud protests.

"Thank you so much for having me here today," Fai said, with great dignity. "And especially for welcoming a stranger to your party just because of the strength of your friendship with my daughter.

"Petra. You are a small intelligent woman who is also very beautiful, and your Ian is a very lucky man. I hope he never imitates you using a high-pitched silly voice, and if he does, I hope you nip that disrespect in the bud. This I have found, is the foundation of a good marriage."

"*Mom.*"

"Shush, Sarah, this is important stuff. You would do well to listen. I have been attending Toastmasters to improve my oratory skills, and you are being rude. Where was I? Of course, the other thing I am thinking of today is mothers and daughters. Because

I am here with my own daughter. Who is not married—but who perhaps will be someday, if she is lucky."

Well, at least the bride-to-be appeared to be enjoying herself again.

That was the nice thing about Jake, Sarah thought, suddenly feeling petulant. He knew that whole history and he was angry on her behalf. Her friends believed her that her mother hadn't always been ideal. But they didn't know it, they didn't feel it, the way Jake did. And it felt so, so comforting to have someone on her side, even when she wasn't sure if she should be on the side she was on. She had a past with Jake—and that was actually very good in some ways.

"Sarah is stubborn," her mother was saying. "I see so much of her in me. And that is why I push her, because it is sometimes like pushing against myself. But even when mothers see clearly about their daughters, it is sometimes hard to just let go. Because that love and fear fight each other even when it seems like they're on the same side.

"Petra is getting married, and in marriage, we parents sometimes think of it as letting go. Even if our children stopped being children long ago. Even if we stopped being proper parents. They don't think they're being let go of."

She looked at Lisa, Petra's mother, directly. Poor Lisa who was maybe a little tipsy herself had started crying.

But Fai looked serene. "What needs release are those visions and thoughts of yourself. I want to think I have worked hard over the years to change myself. I've gone to yoga and taken up parasailing—"

What the—?

"And even joined the town's Toastmasters, although it means listening to other people's speeches. And I was on a trivia team. But sometimes when I see myself—when I see how others see me—I understand it's not quite enough. That all the lessons and getting up early and trying to learn new things don't mean much."

She rubbed her face, and for the first time in a long time, Sarah noticed that her mother seemed tired.

"Another thing about weddings is that sometimes they make you feel old. And after you get as old as me—"

"You're a flexible fox, Mrs. S!" Helen yelled.

Great. Helen was definitely drunk, too.

"Sometimes when you get a little older, you start to have regrets. And that is when you really have to start paying attention, not to the *shouldn't haves*, but to the person you have become and maybe why it has happened. And maybe it is time to forgive yourself and other people. It's a time to learn to at least get along so that you won't have more regrets. So. Letting go doesn't mean abandoning your daughter or your mother, or your sister, or whatever. It means setting aside that anger and sadness and hurt. Sometimes it means letting go of the past."

She raised her glass, and everyone put theirs up.

"To the future," she said.

"To the future," everyone echoed.

Then Fai thumped her glass down and excused herself to the bathroom. Sarah followed a few minutes later and even managed to cluck sympathetically as the sounds of her mother vomiting drifted through the thick, plank door.

CHAPTER EIGHTEEN

Ilse was waiting for Jake when he got back from a run with Mulder.

At first, he thought—hoped—it was Sarah. She had texted him earlier. *Mixing mom with friends,* it said. *Still think this is a good idea?* Attached was a picture of Mrs. Soon in shockingly bright yoga clothing.

Judging by the challenging tone in her text, maybe their dispute wasn't quite over. Then again, arguments were Sarah's version of flirting.

But as the figure on his porch moved out of the shadow, he caught the glint of her hair and felt the disappointment so thick in his throat that it was difficult to reply to Ilse's hello.

She made a move as if to get up and—what, hug him? Kiss him on the cheek?—but before he could ponder the etiquette minefield of how to greet a recent ex-wife who was getting married in a matter of days, Mulder intercepted Ilse's move, put her muddy paws on Ilse's jeans, and sniffed her.

Thank goodness for dogs.

"You grew a beard," she said. Then quickly, "I like this house. Nice neighborhood. Really walkable."

He nodded but didn't try to help the conversation along.

She cleared her throat. "Aren't you going to ask me in?"

He wasn't. Instead, he led her around the back to the plastic patio chairs. He didn't feel like being in the house with her. It was his. Maybe he was being childish, but he didn't want her issues—and she definitely had come to him with something on her mind—crowding his space.

He got her a glass of lemonade, pointed out blankets on the bench in case she got cold. And he informed her he was going in to clean up.

She looked like she was going to say something more. But at his curt nod, she held her tongue.

When he returned, Mulder was lying on her back, squirming ecstatically as Ilse patted her silky belly. Sucker, he thought half affectionately.

"I never even knew you wanted a dog."

"We didn't have time. I put it out of my mind."

He dropped down into a chair.

"We're like two old people," she said, "sitting on a rocking chairs on a porch."

"Minus the rocking chairs. And porch. And the growing old together."

He didn't have to turn to know that she'd blushed bright red. Instead, he stared out at his neighbor, Sandy, who was on a ladder clipping her hedge with a pair of old shears.

He shook his head. "What brings you here, Ilse?"

"I just wanted to talk. It's weird not being able to talk to you. Is your, uh, girlfriend around?"

"No."

"I'd like to meet her."

"That sounds like a disaster."

Sarah's bluntness was definitely rubbing off on him.

Ilse sighed. "Does it have to be like this?"

He looked at her. "Ilse, you showed up unexpectedly at my house fishing for information and obviously wanting something— or to say something. I'm allowed to set my boundaries and decide when I talk to you and what I agree to. And, for that matter, don't you have wedding things to do?"

"You never used to be like this. So—direct."

"Yes, well, we used to be married and now we're not and things change. Probably for the better."

She reeled a little after he said that, too. But he couldn't be sorry. He just couldn't muster up that feeling. He didn't want her to be hurt—not really. A small part of him still felt a twinge of sympathy for her. But he did not want to prolong this, and he was done making himself something else to spare her feelings.

"If things are better—well, you don't seem very happy," she said in a low, familiar tone.

That was the voice she used when they argued. Not that they had raised their voices, because they were both such reasonable people. They were trying to do their very best, so anxious to be the nicest, best spouses to each other. So he used that tone, too. They fretted at each other. It was exhausting just thinking about it.

He closed his eyes.

"I still worry about you, Jake. I still feel guilty. You always said there was no such thing as a clean break. Well, it's true, and maybe I don't want one. I know you don't want to come to the wedding, and I understand it was awkward of me to ask you. But I just want to know that you won't be alone that day. Like, maybe you could go see your dad or something."

So that's why she was here. He was a loose end that she thought was threatening to unravel.

"I won't be alone, Ilse. I'm going to a different wedding. With my girlfriend."

If she was still his girlfriend. God, he hoped she was, because—because the thought of her right now was pushing him. It was giving him strength.

"Oh."

"Other people get married. Their lives move on even though you've never heard of them."

"Jake."

This came out sharply now. She was starting to get frustrated. Welcome to the goddamn club. He had been feeling punchy ever since his confrontation with Mrs. Soon. No, not true. If he had to admit it to himself, this had been a long time in coming. He had just never let it happen before.

But Ilse took a deep breath and tried for a reasonable tone. "Your dad told me a little bit about your girlfriend—"

"Sarah."

"Sarah. She's Winston's sister. You guys didn't talk about her often. You knew her growing up."

"I can't believe you're still speaking with my dad."

"I like the rev. Sometimes we message each other on Facebook. Are you sure this is a good idea? You're going to a wedding with someone so soon after the divorce?"

"Ilse, you're the one who is getting married this very Saturday."

"But I've known Brian for a while now."

"I've known Sarah longer than you've been acquainted with your groom. Sarah and I have seen the worst parts of each other. We haven't always liked each other."

"And now you like her. Can she return your feelings?"

There it was—the knife twist. He liked Sarah—no, it was more than that. But did she feel that way about him? She'd been pushing him away from the start. "I have a lot of feelings for Sarah. I always have."

Ilse was quiet. He sighed. "Ilse, I am tired of being careful around you. I shouldn't have to be now. It didn't end terribly for us—it was very civilized—but now there's this huge … ocean of dark, unspoken stuff between us."

"No, that's not true. It isn't bad. We're friends now. We're *fine*."

"Then why are you here?"

She got up. "It's not bad feelings, per se. That's natural in a marriage to have just a little resentment. A little. Right? After all, you were the one to turn your back on your beliefs. You weren't the nice boy I married. After a couple of years at that job—"

"Don't you dare blame my job. And yes, maybe I stopped being nice, because nice was another word for glossing over the terrible."

"I'm not. I'm not. I guess I should have expected that things wouldn't be exactly the same. And that I would want them to stay that way so much. And that I'd mind so much that my husband had lost his faith because of his work. And how did I know that he wouldn't become disillusioned about me and everything I believe? And then you didn't even fight for me."

She took a deep breath.

"Is that what you wanted?" Jake said after a while.

For the first time, Ilse smiled—albeit shakily. "No. But what did you want?"

Jake didn't answer. She pressed, "You're clearly unhappy about something."

He almost laughed, and she heard it. Because dammit, she still knew him pretty well.

"You got a dog and a girlfriend so quickly. Like you have something to prove."

This time, he did snort. "You had someone lined up before you had me pull the trigger on our marriage. We weren't in love with each other anymore."

At the look on her face, he softened his tone. "Look, it was a hard time for both of us, but it's over and we both survived. Just leave my dog and especially leave my girlfriend out of this."

She shook her head. "I'm sorry. Of course I want you to move on with your life. And of course I keep inviting you because I feel guilty and I want to do something. But I'm here because of both of us. It is possible to be a little selfish and care about another person at the same time."

"Ilse, I wouldn't say I'm happy at precisely this moment. But I feel alive again. Sarah has given me great moments in the last few months. And I wouldn't be happy now with how I used to be—I don't want to go back to what I was. I have moved on."

"With Sarah."

"With Sarah."

She took a deep breath. She nodded. "Does she know how much you love her?"

Ilse did know him pretty well.

"You and Sarah probably agree on one thing—you both think it's too soon. That I don't know my feelings. That is such a fucking insult."

"Jake did you just say—?"

"Yes, I said fucking, already."

Of all the things that were going to push Ilse over the edge: his directness, his refusal to absolve her, his admitting he was in love with someone else—this was the thing that did it.

She gave a little sob at his downward spiral into sin.

"I work with a bunch of potty-mouth kids. I always swore. Just not at home with you."

She wiped her eyes and tried to smile bravely. Or maybe she had been laughing, not crying. "Yes, well, I guess I'll add that to the list of things we didn't share with each other."

"Good luck on Saturday, Ilse," he said.

• • •

Sarah's parents insisted they all wake up early to pick up Winston from the airport. But when they arrived, there was no sign of her brother.

Her father whipped out a pair of Transitions bifocals and began texting. Her mother did the same.

"Are you *both* messaging Winston?"

"Yes," they said at the same time.

Not for the first time, she felt sorry for her asshole brother. But there was nothing to be done about it. She moved off and scanned the arrival times.

Funny, the only flight from Los Angeles had come in an hour ago.

Maybe Winston had built in some extra time before pickup so that he could prepare himself for a parental onslaught. Time enough to soak in copious amounts of alcohol and then spray himself down with Febreze.

Sure enough, ten minutes later, Winston loped up with his luggage. He was wearing a pair of sunglasses that he took off to peck Fai on the cheek. He shook his father's hand. When he got to Sarah, he put his sunglasses back on. "Sis."

"Winston."

They were not a hugging family, and she and Winston had not been close since, well, maybe in elementary school—if ever. Still, they hadn't seen each other in nearly four years. So she made awkward small talk. "How was your flight?"

"Pretty good."

"Cool."

Well. That duty dispensed with, she led them all back to her car and dropped everyone off at the hotel where her mother and father would doubtless attempt to iron and hang up all of Winston's golf shirts.

Sarah felt herself relax after she dropped them off. The atmosphere in the car had been … anticipatory. And not really in a good way. Her mother had said little after her speech at the yoga retreat. Fai had fallen asleep during her massage, and a handsome masseuse named Rick had eventually hauled her out to Sarah's car, but not before they took a group picture with Rick and his dainty, drooling load, flanked by Petra and Helen and the rest of the ladies. Her mother was also quiet—or she was faking unconsciousness—in the car. She did not get up early.

In any case, Sarah had to clear up her patient load before the weekend of revelry, so she spent the rest of the afternoon in the office talking to her patients and clearing up her paperwork. By the next day, she felt tired, but she'd promised to pick up a couple of things for the floral designer and deliver them to Ian and Petra's house. And there was still going to be a pre-wedding gathering to attend tonight.

She wanted to go home and take a nap, but if her parents and Winston were there, there was no way she'd get any rest.

She thought about texting Jake again. That would be a cop-out. They had to talk. She hadn't given much thought to how Winston would react until now, but she suspected that her brother would not have the cockles of his heart warmed by the fact that his childhood best friend was now dating his little sister. The one good thing about Winston's taciturnity was that at least he hadn't berated her in the car. Or maybe he didn't care that she was with Jake. Winston and she weren't children anymore. People changed—as Jake kept on telling her.

She had lived for so many years thinking that she wouldn't have to sit down with her parents or Winston and discuss anything of substance ever again, and it had been painful and blissful at the same time. Well, thanks to Jake, she had been wrong about that.

She was tired, but she did not want to go home. She stretched out in her office and pulled her white coat over her. And it was there Helen found her hours later. "Have you been here this whole time?"

"Oh my god, I have to pick some flower arrangements from Emily."

"Don't worry, Ian called earlier to say she'd already taken them to the restaurant instead. But he couldn't get a hold of you, so he sent me to find you."

Sarah scrubbed her hands with her face. "I have never been undependable in my life. I feel terrible. Is this what it feels like to be a mess?"

"Thanks," Helen said.

"I didn't mean you specifically."

"You fell asleep at your desk, and you have a crease on your cheek. That doesn't mean you're a mess."

"You met my drunk mom, right? And then there's the fact that she now hates my boyfriend who I got mad at for trying to defend me. And the fact that my brother is here and he loathes me. He'll probably try to turn Jake against me."

"That's a new one on me."

"I don't know if it's that I was a brat or if it's because Winston thinks he's got a right to all the attention because he's a boy and he's older—probably a little of both—but we've always had a strained relationship. And now I'm going out with Jake."

"That sounds like Winston's problem and not yours."

"Easily said, but his problem becomes mine as long as he's here talking shit and being taken seriously by my parents and Jake. Let me tell you, it's enough to make me wish that I were going back into OB so that I could have an excuse to disappear on someone else's schedule."

Helen gave her a careful look. "Are you ready to resume your practice?"

"Maybe. I don't know."

They left for Helen's apartment to get changed for the not-a-rehearsal dinner, and Sarah accompanied her friends to the bar. She did not get drunk or feel the urge to get up in front of everyone and wax eloquent. It was a small, well-behaved bunch. Petra's sister, Ellie, and Ellie's girlfriend Jenna sampled wines with the enthusiastic verve of people not far past their twenty-first birthdays. Petra's mom, Lisa, was there with her new boyfriend, James Taylor. Helen cozied herself in a corner with Adam, laughing over something. Joanie was giggling with Petra's sister and her girlfriend. And Petra and Ian were at the center of it all, looking happier and more relaxed than two people who were entering a legally binding lifetime commitment the next day had a right to look. Sarah wasn't sure how she felt about Petra getting married, about her family, and most of all about Jake. But she felt his absence.

The party broke up early. They still had a lot to do the next day. And Sarah returned to her quiet house and her quiet bed and stayed awake for most of the night because she'd slept too long in her office.

At 1:00 a.m. she called Jake.

He answered as if it hadn't been nearly a week since they'd talked. "Did you have a good time at your rehearsal dinner?"

"It was fine."

I wish you'd been there, she wanted to say.

Instead, she said, "We're still on for tomorrow?"

"Are you sure you want me to come with you?"

"Yes, I want you to come with me. I never said I didn't."

"Sarah," he sighed, and she did not cry at all the longing in his voice, although she wanted to.

There was just too much to think about right now. Her best friend was getting married. She was going to have to make a decision about her work. Her parents were here and their need to talk hung heavily over her; her brother was here and he wanted the opposite. And she wanted to lean on Jake. She wanted to trust him because not having anyone else to trust wasn't working anymore. "It's late, and I don't think we should get into it right now."

"Of course, you're right."

"We're both right."

But after he hung up, she couldn't sleep.

• • •

The downpour started early in the morning. By noon, Sarah, Helen, and Helen's boyfriend Adam had tracked down all the guests to make sure they knew that the wedding would be held at Ian's restaurant instead of in the park. The rain and change of venue hadn't been completely unexpected—this was Portland. And Ian and Petra seemed calm as they directed the proceedings.

That was marriage, after all, wasn't it? Going through the bumps and trying to smooth them with four hands instead of two? Sure the plan was that they'd be together and file their taxes jointly. It was practical, probably.

Sarah had never given much thought about living with someone, having a wedding, or husbands, for that matter. She'd assumed she'd be alone. Not that she thought she was damaged goods or anything like that. It was more that she'd assumed that like with anything involving serious familial ties, she would never get to be herself. A husband would tell her what to be, what to do. And she'd be trapped by that idea.

It was strange, because her father was hardly like that. Her parents respected each other. They let each other be their own person. She was surprised that that had never occurred to her before. Or maybe she never expected to find that for herself.

Jake had gotten married. He had been a husband. Somehow, he didn't make that word seem so bad either.

But a lot of the men she knew wanted to be married. They were intent on securing their own spouses and getting children and cushioning themselves with people and family. And quite honestly, marriage was so great for men. They received all that affection and support, and they were admired for wanting commitment and love. If she confessed to the same needs, she would be met with a different reaction.

But she'd gone out with men who wanted weddings and kids, and they all assumed it was what she wanted, too—she delivered babies, after all. Her parents had been together for a long time, and maybe it was because she was so used to seeing them as united against her and Winston that she still didn't think of them as models of nuptial bliss so much as they were a gale force.

Seeing Ian and Petra in action together, marriage almost seemed … possible. The way Petra smoothed Ian's brow when he got frazzled, the way Ian made Petra laugh. The way Petra still managed to be herself in their relationship—but a happier, more energetic version of herself than Sarah had ever seen.

Jake could be like that for her, an errant thought whispered.

But mostly she was too busy picking up favors from the apartment, heading over to Ian's restaurant Field to pitch in for whatever needed to be done. It was good to feel needed and good to work with all of her friends and Ian's staff. She was like her parents in a lot of ways. She had trouble sitting still.

By afternoon, the restaurant was transformed. It was funny. She'd been here many times thanks to Petra. Field's dark polished wood and copper fixtures had become familiar to her, but this place now seemed soaring and spacious. Ian and his crew had been busy. They'd taken out many of the chairs and tables—Sarah speculated they were piled up in Ian's basement office. And there were more flowers than she'd ever seen. Ranunculus, the floral designer called them, frilled like petticoats, waving exuberantly in mason jars on the tables, sweet peas and ornamental cabbage or kale dotting the wide aisle where Petra would be walking, leading up to the space at the front where Ian would be waiting with the officiant. Later, a patch of floor would be cleared for dancing. And now, the ceiling was decorated with what seemed like thousands of little lights. It made everything seem higher, almost as if the sky were above them. It was strange that the place, even filled with people she knew, suddenly seemed so much bigger.

As if by agreement, they all stood still to gaze at it for a moment.

Guests would be arriving in a few hours, and eating and laughing, and the room wouldn't be quiet anymore.

Petra, her face and hair fancied up, brought a glass of champagne over to her and Helen. They toasted silently and swallowed.

"Bubbles are sort of tickling my nose and eyes," Helen muttered, swiping her hand over her face.

"Shut it, you big softie," Petra said, dabbing carefully at her makeup.

Sarah didn't say anything. Her voice wasn't quite there anymore.

She got up and hugged her two dearest friends in the world, and they stood there for a minute longer before someone unplugged the white lights and the room exploded into motion again.

CHAPTER NINETEEN

So this is what prom is like, Jake thought as he waited in Sarah's living room with Mr. and Mrs. Soon. It was humid and he was in a suit. He had reason to be unnerved. He hadn't seen Sarah in days, and their chat last night had been guarded. Somewhere across town, his ex-wife was exchanging vows and rings with some nice, affection-stealing man who was everything that Jake used to be. And he wasn't angry about that, but he was bothered by the fact that Sarah's parents were silently gazing at him like a pair of cats contemplating a trapped mouse.

"Where's Winston?" he asked, finally.

The parents gave identical looks of amazement that he had chosen to speak. "He said he had some work to do."

"Distance cosmetic dentistry?" Jake asked, frowning.

"I'm sure it is something important."

Jake was sure it was not. Winston had his own interesting ways of ascertaining that he wouldn't have to spend that much time with his family even while loudly proclaiming that he was. Winston could act like he was doing his duty without actually having to talk to his parents or be around. Or host them. In his home. Interesting how he managed to get away with that.

There was a step in the hall, and then Sarah appeared.

Jake sucked in a breath and promptly forgot all of his worries.

He was aware that he was a little slack-jawed but he lacked the ability to close his mouth. Also, he didn't care, because Sarah glowed in front of him like a sun, and he knew that he had to open every part of his being to absorb her into his pores. Somehow he managed to get to his feet. Somehow once he got to his feet, he managed cross the room and put both his hands out to her and take hers. And once her fingers closed firmly around his, he wanted more warmth. He wanted to carry her away into a bower, or a garden, or some lush, verdant place, filled with gently flitting butterflies and fountains and maybe a maze, and set her down gently on a bench and soak her in and smooth his hands up her legs.

Higher.

He wrenched his mind away from that thought.

She was wearing green, a lovely, slim lacy green dress that was somehow demure and fresh and old-fashioned. Her hair was up and soft looking, adorned with a white rose. And she had on a few small silver bangles. His thumb crept over her wrists, and he made them jangle faintly.

She was everything he had ever wanted and many things he never knew he'd wanted.

Mrs. Soon took a picture of them, standing slightly apart with their hands together, looking at each other. She didn't urge them closer together. She didn't even really say much. She just watched them.

Jake didn't care what she thought. Which was getting to be a problem.

Sarah cleared her throat. "Don't wait up," she said to her parents.

It was supposed to be a joke, probably. But she looked serious.

He *felt* serious.

With great care, he took her arm, and it was so light and warm and strong. They gazed at each other solemnly and walked out of the house, but because he was so busy being earnest, he forgot about the rain. The cold splash startled him, and Sarah's laughter woke him up enough to send him back for an umbrella.

He escorted her to his newly cleaned car, shut the door and made his way around to the driver's seat. But he didn't put his key in the ignition. He couldn't.

"You look—you look … no, you are the most fresh, beautiful, incandescent person," he said. "So damn perfect."

She smiled, such a small smile, and his heart gave a little twist.

But her words were light. "I'm beginning to think that weddings make you sloppy, Mr. Li."

"I brought a bunch of tissues just in case."

He started the engine.

"You look handsome," she said quietly, so quietly that he almost didn't hear it.

She wasn't even looking at him when she said it.

Weddings did make him feel sloppy, though. Or maybe it was being buttoned up tight in his suit, his hair and beard smoothed down, with Sarah seeming subdued next to him in the car as they drove there that made him want to burst out. He wanted to tell her they should skip it. They should drive and keep on driving until they got to California, changed their names to Sven and Nancy, and didn't have to deal with mothers, fathers, brothers, or exes.

Ilse was wrong. It was going to be a great weekend for him *because* she was getting married and Petra and Ian were getting married, and there—right there—was the triumph of hope. Maybe his past love hadn't lasted forever, but that didn't mean the future would be terrible.

As if sensing his shifting feelings, Sarah turned to him and put her hand on his knee. "I'm glad you're with me," she said.

And even though she was not acting like her usual self—and maybe a part of him should be even more worried about the sadness of her tone—most of him was just so happy and relieved at her words, happy to be carried on his current euphoria, that he covered her hand and didn't take it off again until they pulled into a parking space downtown.

Plus, he was going to take her back home and they were going to screw. If that wasn't a reason to look forward to the future, he didn't know what was.

He was grinning from ear to ear as Sarah reintroduced him to her friends. Dark-haired Helen was nestled within the arms of Adam, who had been a professional hockey player for Portland. Jake had only been dimly aware that Portland had a team. There'd been some sort of controversy about a canceled arena, he recalled. Adam was starting graduate school for social work now, so he and Jake had something to talk about. Petra was apparently with her sister and mother, being fussed over. Ian, the groom, was doing some last minute directing. He appeared a little harried—which, considering the circumstances, was natural. Jake sent him a sympathetic grin, too, aware that he was probably looking too happy and maybe a little drunk, even though he hadn't had any alcohol yet.

On cue, a waiter swooped by with champagne. Indoor weddings at restaurants really were the best.

He took one for Sarah and one for himself and drained the glass quickly.

Sarah shot him a frown, but he didn't care. He was damn happy to be with her, and he squeezed her so that she knew it.

"Take it easy," she murmured.

"I've only had one glass."

"I mean on the happiness. Everyone is going to start thinking you're the groom."

"Please, I was never this delighted when I was the groom."

She sent him a narrow look. "What is that supposed to mean?"

"Everyone stares at you when you're the husband-to-be. And makes bad jokes about balls and chains."

"So toxic masculinity is a bitch."

"I can't begin to unpack that statement right now."

A little after 5:00 p.m., a jazz trio struck up the opening vamp of "My Baby Just Cares for Me." Sarah's friend Petra walked in, her face shining with joy and maybe some relief.

"She looks happier than I did," he whispered to Sarah.

"Oh, hush."

He hadn't expected Sarah to really cry—he hadn't really expected to feel anything himself. But between handing her tissues and listening to the officiant, he felt a swell of something more begin deep down in his body.

But Sarah sat beaming as she watched her friend. She was fiercely and magnificently proud, but also a little overwhelmed, like she wasn't sure how to deal with what she was seeing. And it hurt to look at Sarah tearing up, even if it was for joy. It hurt like a flower taking root and blossoming in his chest, and he couldn't stop gazing at her, even though he was supposed to be staring at the bride and groom.

Something of what he was feeling probably showed in his face, because when she accepted another tissue from him, she smiled at him and whispered. "I'm a bit weirded out is all. It's not often that you see your best friend decked out in finery and performing sentimental dinner theater."

He would have replied, but it was time to exchange vows.

And then Petra and Ian kissed and the guests cheered. There was a buzz of confusion when the photographer asked everyone to group together for a picture. Hockey player Adam, he noticed, also looked a little dazzled and teary as Helen herded him to the back.

He grabbed Sarah's arm and followed them. "What did you mean you were weirded out?"

She thought for a minute. "I see Petra every day. But I almost don't recognize her. And she's up there, small and at a distance, and

I almost want to run up and help her. I'm a lot more emotionally invested in this than I thought I would be."

"It's strange," Helen agreed. "I don't think I realized that anything was going to change until I saw Petra appear in her dress." She turned to her boyfriend and reached up to touch his face. "Are you okay?" she murmured.

"I love weddings," Adam said helplessly.

The photographer was on a ladder, yelling instructions at everyone to squeeze in together. Sarah and Helen and he and Adam formed a tight knot. The photographer counted down to three, and the crowd gave a huge whoop.

"And let's take another. This time with the bride and groom in the middle!" the photographer yelled.

More squishing and more posing and another deafening roar, and everyone was allowed to go and take their seats.

"How are *you* feeling?" Adam asked him as they pulled out their chairs. "I'm feeling all sorts of sentimental. Something about all the beautiful flowers and people dancing and the food—"

"And the champagne."

"And the bubbly. And people you love coming out as the most beautiful and radiant versions of themselves, getting up and gazing deeply at each other to make these sincere vows. It just gets to me." Adam seemed to be getting more and more misty-eyed. "I just love her," he said, his gaze snagging on Helen. "And I'm really happy. That's all."

"You've got wedding fever."

"I do."

"God, don't say *I do* to me."

"Can't blame a guy for trying."

They laughed, and it occurred to Jake that he and Adam could be friends, and also that perhaps he and Adam were well on their way to getting very drunk.

Ian had apparently arranged to cater some of the dinner with a food truck parked outside the restaurant. The rain let up just a little bit, so small groups of happy guests could dash out and breathe in the cooling air from the outside, holding their jackets over their heads while they waited for small paper boats filled with hot samosas and grilled paneer. There was a small dance floor and the band in the corner. It was a little chaotic, a little loud, and perfect. Jake had loosened his tie, rolled up his sleeves, and lost his jacket. And now he was out with the crowd, swaying to the music with Sarah. They'd never danced together—thirty years of knowing each other, and he'd never held her on a dance floor. He wished they'd done it earlier.

"You've got a look in your eye that I don't quite trust," she said.

"Are you afraid I'm going to do this?" He swung her around deftly, and she gasped. "Or this?"

He took her into a low dip, and this time she squealed.

"Ugh, bring me up again!"

He pulled her up laughing, and there was a spatter of applause from nearby friends. Her face was red, and she looked a little disheveled and far too sexy. He smoothed her hair back.

"So what were you afraid I was going to do?" he whispered when he had her back upright and safe.

"Mmm. Nothing. It's nothing."

"It's definitely something."

"No, I was just afraid you might try to do something foolish."

"Like what?"

"Persistent, aren't you. Come on, let's get some water or something."

"What were you going to say, Sarah?"

She sighed. "Let's not do this right now. Let's sit down. We've all had a little bit to drink—"

"You haven't really."

She ignored him. "Emotions are running high. They haven't even cut the cake yet."

"Just tell me."

She shook her head. "I don't know. You have this look like you want to make some sort of declaration."

• • •

It was the right thing to say. Maybe. Except that perhaps Sarah could have delivered her message a little more tactfully.

Story. Of. Her. Life.

"First of all, I didn't know that 'making a declaration' was a look—or maybe you've just had so damn many men fall at your feet."

"We are not going to go into my dating history, Jake."

"Believe me, we're not. But second, is that the worst thing? If I did tell you I loved you? Or proposed."

"No, but it would be impulsive."

"And God knows we should all keep our wits about us when we're in love."

She winced. "I know that the atmosphere here is very romantic—I mean, I help set it up. If this wedding can't make me believe in love, then nothing will. But this is not the time, Jake. It's … this is the weekend that your ex-wife is getting married. We haven't been going out that long. This is your first relationship after your divorce. We haven't really talked anything through."

"Your mom has already mentioned marriage."

"Bringing Ma Soon into it does not help your case, buddy."

"And I'm not the only one who's thinking of it. Adam over there has visions of tulle dancing in his head."

"Adam and Helen have been living together for half a year, and they've at least had a conversation or two about it. Plus, there's the fact that you are somewhat tipsy."

She would have added more, but Helen barreled in between them. "Hey, you two, they're getting ready to cut the cake."

He *had* been thinking of saying something drunken and dramatic. It wasn't only the blurry look in a face softened by alcohol. It was the way he held her—she knew he was going to say something. She'd burst his bubble, and a small part of her felt cruel because he had been so happy. But he wasn't ready for this.

More importantly, she wasn't ready for this.

She was feeling five hundred sorts of vulnerable. She was afraid she'd yield or crumble and it would be for all the wrong reasons.

He had moved away from her to watch Petra and Ian. They held the knife together, poised over the cake. Oddly enough, it was in that moment when he concentrated fiercely on not looking at her that she saw all of his longing come into his face, just before the guests gave their shout of approval and the knife slid through the beautiful surface of the icing, bringing down a mess of crumbs and sticky frosting. She felt his feelings push through her, right through her chest and down her middle.

But Jake was not giving up so quickly. After they sat back down at their table, he continued. "You're pushing me away again."

"I have a good reason this time."

"No, you don't. So what if I was thinking about at least talking about marriage with you? It's a wedding. That's what happens. People are getting married, and it makes me think of marriage. I'm not going to get down on bended knee right now, but I want to talk about it."

"You've been drinking."

"Drinking is the perfect time to say what you're really feeling. Because you just pour everything out without inhibition. This," he said, waving one hand at himself, "this is my heart. On my sleeve."

She glanced obediently at the spot where he gestured, and her gaze traveled up his sinewy forearms. They were indeed compelling. She cleared her throat and tried to focus. "Jake, your sleeves are rolled up."

This fact did not slow him. "Sarah Soon, I love you. I want to tell the world. Or at least this table."

She felt a flash of happiness, a bright beacon of euphoria that was quickly engulfed by fear.

He turned to the people sitting with them. "I want to propose a toast. *To love!*"

"Hear, hear!" Adam cheered.

Jake raised his glass. "I was not expecting this, to feel anything. I was fully prepared to not feel anything for a long time. Get through the day. Get through my work. I thought the best that I could do was live. And then there you were, more alive and vibrant, than anyone I'd ever seen."

It was too much—too much love, too much generosity. She wanted to listen, put her hands on his face and have him tell her all of this. But she wanted to stop him, too, because her feelings had been jumbled all day and she was terrified. She could not possibly live up to his vision of her.

"I love this woman. I love her mouthiness and the fact that she has never been shy about telling me and everyone else exactly how she feels. I love you even when you're angry, Sarah, because when you are angry, it is a mark of how deeply you care about something—about everything. Sarah Soon, you have no idea how good you are."

"Please," Helen muttered, "Sarah thinks the world of herself."

But Jake heard her and turned to her. "No, she's always trying and never satisfied—she's always wanting herself and others to improve. That's a mark that she always thinks she has to do better, not that she thinks she's good. But does she appreciate how good she is already? I don't know if she does. I am trying to be good enough for the person she already is. And I am glad that she is letting me grow."

Even Helen was quiet after that. Then she held up her glass. "To my beautiful friends," she said.

They all drank. Even Sarah, who wasn't sure what to do with herself or what to say. She could feel the heaviness of tears behind her eyes. Again.

Fucking weddings.

Jake leaned in and whispered. "I love you, and I want you to know it. I want you to know that you are wonderful and good," he whispered.

She shook her head. She wanted to be these things, but right now she felt like a mess. "It doesn't matter how good I try to be—"

"It does."

"I fail all the time. My body is fallible. I'm still human."

"It matters," he said fiercely.

She took a deep drink of champagne and willed herself not to say anything more. But he hiccupped and turned. Adam leaned over and patted him sympathetically. "That was so beautiful."

Jake wiped away the tears in his eyes that she'd been afraid to shed.

"Men are emotional wrecks," Helen said.

"We need to cut them off," Sarah answered roughly.

A waiter came by. "More champagne?"

"Yes!" Adam and Jake chorused.

"NO!" Helen and Sarah shouted at the same time.

The waiter took in Jake's strong forearms and former-pro hockey player Adam's bulk. Then he shifted his gaze to Helen and Sarah.

He knew who was scarier. He backed away with a nervous smile.

The Maudlin Brothers pouted until they were served their cake. Then they began talking about graduate programs in social work and managed a sloppy exchange of phone numbers. Helen interjected a couple of times to help them along, pleased at their budding friendship. But Sarah didn't know what to do with herself and how to feel. She loved Jake. She hadn't said it back, but he didn't need her to say it—and she loved him for that, too. But her emotions had gone up and down and sideways all day, and she was overwhelmed.

Most of all, she couldn't stop thinking about what he'd said.

She had lost confidence in her abilities—no, it wasn't that exactly. She had lost confidence that ability had anything to do with it keeping her patients safe and alive—keeping her friends, keeping herself that way. And maybe these little tasks and quests that she'd been on for the last few months had been an attempt to prove that what she did mattered, even if she'd lost most of her faith in herself.

Jake believed in her. He saw her. His belief in her was almost casual in the way he didn't even question it. He'd made a speech, and now he was chatting with Adam and eating cake. It was as if loving her was just a normal, easy thing for him.

God, that kind of trust was frightening.

As if responding to her thoughts, he gave her knee a squeeze, and tears welled up in her eyes again at the affection of it. It was moving—and terrifying to be the object of this amount of love. She could only sit there moving as little as possible for fear that more of her feelings and sobs would spill all over and around her.

Jake and Adam weren't the only ones who had fallen under the spell of jazz, flowers, and samosas. Because as the band took a short break, a man at the head table stood up. "Lisa Lale," said Petra's mom's date. "You are the most wonderful, precious woman I have ever met. This has been a magical night, and your daughters are amazing people. No wonder you are so proud of them."

James Taylor was a red-faced man with a bushy beard. He looked happy, kind, and permanently bewildered. But there was no mistaking the glint in his eye. "I can't wait another minute longer to say how much I care about you. I love you. Will you marry me?"

"Oh my gosh," Lisa squealed. "Yes, James, I don't want to waste any more of my life."

"Oh shit," the bride said distinctly through a mouthful of cake.

CHAPTER TWENTY

Sarah drove Jake home and bundled him upstairs to bed. He made an effort to keep her there with him, but she was tired and needed to think, and he muddled her brain.

Plus, she had been around people all day—managing them all day. At least she and Helen hadn't had to step in after Petra's mom's abrupt engagement. Ian had been quick and effective in soothing his new wife's worries. That boded well for their marriage.

But now, Sarah was looking forward to having some time alone—at least that's what she told herself. So she helped Jake take off his jacket, put a bottle of aspirin and a big glass of water by his bed, gave Mulder a pat, and drove herself home to be alone.

But her driveway was full of cars, and judging by the lights blazing from her windows, her parents were up.

Winston was there. As well as a blond woman who appeared tired and annoyed—although she was trying to hide it.

"This is your brother's girlfriend, Kirsten," Mr. Soon explained.

Sarah said hello, and Kirsten unbent to flash her a strained smile.

"Erm, what's going on?" Sarah asked even though after the night she'd had, she was afraid of the answer.

It didn't look like there'd been yelling—just … tension. For all Sarah could tell, they all could have been glaring at each other for the last two minutes or the last two hours.

"Not that I'm not glad to meet you, Kirsten, but why is everyone here?"

"Winston is not staying in that—a *hotel*. With Kirsten."

In other words, they didn't want Winston sleeping—or sleeping—in the same bed as his girlfriend, and Winston di have the guts to stand up to his parents and spare Kirsten spectacle. Sarah's gaze moved from her mother to Kirsten Winston—who was hovering protectively over her.

"How did you all end up here?" Sarah asked.

Her father said, "We wanted to take Winston out to dinner thought we would explore a bit. But Winston did not answer of our texts, so we became worried. We took our car to his h and your mother went up and knocked on his door and no ans\

"And then?"

"And then what could we do? We looked for long, long for a place to park. Too expensive everywhere, but finally mother saw a place behind us on the one-way street and she out and stood in the parking spot and saved it until I got aro again."

"A driver tried to take it from me, but I stood there,' mother added.

"And then we decided to find a place for dinner. It to long. So we texted again and again. Then we ate anyway and back to the hotel."

"And your brother came into the bar, all messy, and *kissing* Kirsten. So we introduced ourselves."

Hoo boy.

She could sense that her mother was struggling to herself. If Sarah weren't tired and feeling crowded in I house, she might have enjoyed the show. "Okay, so—uh-Kirsten here right now?"

"We are getting to know her," her mother said tightly

"It's one in the morning."

"*Good point.* I have the rental car. I'm going to driv back to the hotel," Winston said.

"No, you are not," his mother said.

"Jesus, I'll come back here."

He got a glare for taking the Lord's name in vain. "No more funny business. Your dad will drive her."

"Dad has trouble driving at night. And he's in a city."

"How considerate of you, Winston," Sarah couldn't help saying.

"Sarah, you will drive her."

Sarah shut her mouth and tried not to sink down where she stood. She was exhausted, and she was damn sick of dealing with them.

"How about we all stay here?"

"There isn't enough room."

"Or I can go to Jake's. He lives less than five minutes away."

It was funny how easy it was to say it—how good it was. She could just go to his place and be away from all this drama that her family drummed up over nothing.

She could trust him to take her in even when he was in a drunken sleep.

"Winston can stay with Jake."

"Listen," Sarah said in her best doctor voice. "It's late. Everyone's tired. All of this getting to know each other can hold till morning. I am going to make suggestions. Ma and Pa Soon, you do your thing. Winston, there are linens in the closet. You can take the couch, or ... whatever. It's not my business. Kirsten, you are very welcome to stay in the guest room that I've been sleeping in—but if you'd rather not, here's a number for a cab."

"*I* will drive Kirsten wherever she wants." Winston's voice held a faintly pleading quality as he looked at his girlfriend. And suddenly Sarah felt just a bit sorry for her brother.

Just a bit.

"Fine. You're grown-ups—apparently. You sort yourselves out. I'm also a grown-up, and I'm really, really tired. I'm going to Jake's. I have his car anyway."

No one said anything this time.

...

Jake downed aspirin and the bottle of water Sarah handed him while she gave him a quick sketch of what had happened the night before. In truth, he didn't have a hangover. He felt great, because even though he hadn't known it, she'd spent the night.

She did not address his wedding speech.

However, it was pretty clear that she hadn't slept much and was still tired. Jake was nearly shaking with impatience to talk to her about his impromptu declaration, but they would have plenty of time to hash it out later. Right now, they had to present a united front.

The Soons were not a brunching people. Jake and Sarah showed up early for a Sunday—8:00 a.m.—but Sarah's dad was already out in the front yard weeding, and when they got to the dining room, there was a vase of fresh cut flowers, and a new, orange plasticky-looking table runner that, no doubt, her mom had bought at a bargain store to protect the wood. There was also a huge pot of some sort of brown rice and steel cut oatmeal porridge, tiny saucers of hot pickled bamboo, peanuts, pepitas, dried seaweed, sriracha, goji berries, and cut up apples and pears.

"This is sort of random," Jake said, nonetheless helping himself to porridge and sprinkling pepitas over everything.

"You know my parents, always trying to make things healthy."

"Where's Mom?" Sarah asked Winston, who was sitting at the table surrounded by a few more empty bowls.

"I don't know."

It seemed that he'd eaten all the eggs and the smoked salmon.

But he looked terrible, so Jake didn't say anything about it. Apparently Sarah felt the same. With some effort, she slid a smile over her face. "So. How are you doing?"

"I'm fine, okay?"

"And your girlfriend? She's feeling all right about all of this?"

He glared at her, and Jake tensed.

"Sarah Perfect again. Does the wrong thing and still gets welcomed into the fold. You even spent the night with Jake, and Mom and Dad didn't say anything. While I had to sleep on your short, lumpy couch."

"You didn't have to do anything you didn't want to, Win," Sarah said from between gritted teeth.

Jake wanted to smack him. Instead, he said, "Hey, Winston. Hey. Try not to be a jerk, all right?"

"Now you've got him twisted around your finger, thinking he can defend you all the time," Winston said.

"Please. The only reason there's a difference to how they treated us last night is because you ignored their texts and tried to sneak Kirsten to town and into your hotel room. I was at least open about going to Jake's. I'm not saying that Ma and Pa handled this well at all—they are clearly working against their impulses. But at least they're … changing?"

"People don't change, Sarah."

"I have to hope that they can, Winston."

Winston turned to his old friend. "I remember when she used to make fun of you, Jake. She called you a Goody Two-shoes. She laughed with her swim team friends when one of them said I'd die a virgin. They said that you would, too."

"Well, I guess we've taken care of that," Jake said.

It was a crude strike—hitting both Sarah and Winston the wrong way. But Jake's mouth didn't feel like working. Winston's words hung in the charged air bringing to life all of Jake's own ugly memories of high school. Sarah kept her eyes down, and he hardly wanted to look at her.

She'd said all that stuff years and years ago. They'd been different people. Hadn't he been hoping Sarah would put all of this behind her?

He still felt hurt, though. Out of the corner of his eye, he saw her raise her head to say something—to Winston. Not a word to him to explain or apologize. But a woman who Jake assumed was Kirsten chose that moment to walk in.

She looked warily at all of them. The room vibrated with tension. But Kirsten quickly put on a smile and introduced herself to him. She couldn't have slept well.

"What are we fighting about now?" Kirsten asked, taking in Winston's tense grip on the coffee spoon and Jake's glare.

Sarah still hadn't looked at him.

"Nothing," Sarah said, her voice sounding so normal. "It's nothing we're going to get into before everyone is properly fed and caffeinated. Kirsten, would you like a cup? There's milk and soymilk in the fridge. The sugar bowl is over there. And we have stevia."

"I'll take sugar, thanks. We're still divided about the benefits of stevia."

"Everyone got the stevia memo except me."

"I'm a nutritionist."

"I was going to introduce her—that was the plan," Winston muttered. "I was just trying to ease everyone into it."

"We do take some getting used to," Sarah said, more to Kirsten than to her brother—or to Jake.

She still wasn't talking to him. He wasn't sure he could speak to her.

• • •

Jake was hurt. His jaw was tense, and his slumberous eyes were almost completely closed. She knew he was trying to tamp down his feelings, and she needed to apologize right now. She had to get Jake away from this table, from Winston, and from this goddamn stevia.

The worst part was that she remembered those comments. She *had* laughed about it with her so-called friends. It hadn't been funny, but she had gone along, and later those same people had turned against her. Then she'd railed against Jake for not defending her. She'd carried that grudge until that night they'd met up to get reacquainted. She had pounded on the scarred table in the sushi restaurant asking her why he hadn't been a better friend, doubting that he had changed. But he'd apologized sincerely and promptly.

What had she done? How could she have forgotten so conveniently that she'd done similar things to him?

The memory filled her with shame. She knew she wouldn't go along with that kind of talk now. But that was grown-up Sarah who knew it—the woman who eventually felt that same sting of contempt from those friends. She'd had to live through it in order to learn it. Past Sarah had been selfish and cowardly.

She needed to pull Jake away and talk to him. But first, she was going to kill Winston.

She turned to him, ready to give him a piece of her mind, when Jake got up abruptly and stalked to the kitchen.

She half rose, too, muttering to her brother, "At least give Kirsten some fruit, dickwad, instead of eating it all yourself. Just because the bowl is closer to you doesn't mean you own it."

"No thanks," Kirsten said. "I'm good."

Winston stuck out his tongue at her and stuffed a slice of apple in his mouth.

Don't get distracted. Go to Jake. But old habits died hard. "At least pass some fruit over."

"Get it yourself."

At the last minute, he shoved the bowl across the table, and it slid right across her dining room table, past their shocked faces, and shattered on the floor, scattering apple and pear and glass shards everywhere.

There was a silence.

"Winston!"

That was Kirsten. She had sprung up. Jake emerged from the kitchen and blinked at the wreckage. There was a short pause, then he started picking up the bigger, jagged pieces, carrying them carefully to the kitchen garbage.

"I didn't mean to do it."

Winston sounded like a little boy.

"That was my bowl!"

Sarah knew she sounded like a plaintive child herself. But she couldn't help it. He'd smashed her crockery and ruined the fruit, and all because he was a spiteful jerk.

Then Winston stood up and said, "Well, you should've caught it."

That was it.

She just couldn't hold back anymore. She went at him with a yell and punched her brother right in his egg and salmon-filled face.

Winston looked shocked. And also remarkably not bloodied. Maybe he was made of rocks, which proved once and for all that she wasn't related to him. Or maybe he'd eaten rocks, because *yikes!* his face had hurt her fist.

There was a silence. Then Winston yowled and grabbed his glass of water and dashed it in her face with a flourish worthy of a soap star.

She gasped—or was that Kirsten? No time to check if there were casualties. She grabbed the seaweed and dumped the bowl on her brother's head and threw her own water glass at him so that dark strips wallpapered his shirt.

Meanwhile, Winston was frantically lobbing spoonfuls of oatmeal at her, grabbing whatever plates were in reach—snatching the one from his girlfriend's unwilling hands without a word of thanks—and flinging handfuls of pepitas in Sarah's face to distract her.

That meant war. She lobbed peanuts at him as she chased him awkwardly around the kitchen table.

Kirsten was shrieking about something—her breakfast maybe? Or the broken bowl still in pieces on the ground? Or maybe the glob of oatmeal in hair she'd painstakingly styled in order to meet the family?

Dimly, Sarah was aware that Jake had returned from the kitchen again and was also yelling. She tried to slow down and calm down, because she had things to say to him. The situation was out of hand, and she wanted to stop it right there. But as she started toward him, she stepped in a mushy puddle of porridge and started to flail. She grabbed at the table, but that proved a mistake, because although she managed to stay upright, the new orange tablecloth proved slippery. Everything—flowers, empty and full dishes, plates, coffee—everything came down in a magnificent crash and tinkle on the floor around her.

A plate spun in the corner and fell over, spun and stopped.

Another silence.

Her parents chose that moment to appear in the doorway. Mrs. Soon was wearing hot pink yoga pants and a slim-fitting yellow top, and Sarah's eyes hurt a little bit, but whether it was from the colors or from seeing her mom in more formfitting clothing, Sarah didn't know. She'd just never get used to it. Her dad was in his usual uniform of khakis and a polo shirt, and he was streaked with dirt.

Then again, it probably wasn't Sarah's place to judge based on appearances right now. The Soons looked first at the floor, then up at their food-smeared thirty-something progeny, then at Kirsten, whose shoulders were shaking silently, whether from laughter or because she was sobbing, it was hard to tell. Then they moved their eyes to Jake—the only one of them who was still clean.

Finally, Mrs. Soon stirred. She went to Kirsten and led her gently out of the room, murmuring something about helping her get the porridge out of her hair. Mr. Soon shook his head. "Winston. Sarah. I think it's time you clean up your own messes."

And he turned on his heel and went back out the door.

CHAPTER TWENTY-ONE

There was oatmeal on the ceiling and on the light fixture.

Jake and Sarah worked silently, sweeping up the broken glass and food, scrubbing the walls and mopping the floors.

Winston had helped a little at first, too, but then Mrs. Soon had come in and told her son that Kirsten had left. She'd called a cab and departed for the hotel or the airport—Mrs. Soon couldn't say. Winston had yelled at his mother, maybe for the first time ever, and run out the door. Fai Soon hadn't stopped him.

Jake swiped the table angrily.

"I'm sorry," Sarah said.

"Are you okay?" he asked, not acknowledging her apology.

She grimaced. "I need some ice for my hand."

He rummaged around the freezer and found a stack of medical ice packs.

They sat on the floor side by side. "You should have said something earlier," he told her. "I'd have cleaned up."

"Like you clean up everything."

She glanced around the room, and he followed her gaze. It was mostly restored to order. A lone bottle of sweetener stood on the table. "Figures that the only thing we didn't break was that stupid controversial stevia that no one is going to use."

Sarah started to laugh, and even though the sadness of that sound pinched his sore heart, he laughed with her. "You could always upend it on Winston when he comes back. Sort of like a finishing glaze."

"Ooh, I can't believe I punched him in the face," she said burying her head in her hands. "Well, it was sort of a punch. I guess I can add socking Winston to the list of things I've never done and always wanted to do, and then cross it off."

"I find it hard to believe you've never hit Winston."

"As a kid, sure, but never in the face. Have you ever punched him?"

"I have. But I'm still sort of jealous that you got to do it, because I've really felt like taking a swing lately."

"If it's any consolation, it was a weak effort."

"Punching is probably the only thing Sarah Soon doesn't do well."

"Jake, in case you haven't seen this room, or, like, my life, there are a lot of things I don't do well. I don't even understand how you want to be a part of all of this mess. I'm not just talking about breakfast. I mean all of this family. You're going to feel like you have to clean up every time. Kirsten did not want to be around us, and I totally understand that. My family is difficult. And I'm treating myself like I had a brush with death."

"You did."

"Maybe. But apologizing is also something I don't do well. Jake—

"Don't. Don't give me that pitying look."

"It's not pity."

But before she could say more, the door slammed, Winston strode through into the dining room, and she turned away. Again.

That was the problem.

Winston was fuming. And his eye was beginning to bruise. Jake would have congratulated Sarah for hitting him harder than she thought, but then Winston pointed at his sister. "Kirsten's gone, and this is your fault."

Jake got up from the floor. He was getting tired of being interrupted by the Soons.

"What happened?" Sarah asked before Jake could say anything.

"She said she was humiliated by everything that happened and that she didn't want to be around someone as immature as I am."

"I'm sorry, Winston."

Jake interrupted. "You don't need to say you're sorry, Sarah. This isn't your fault. This is his damn fault."

"Or it's mine," said Mrs. Soon, behind Winston.

Kau Soon came in and stood behind his wife.

"I am sorry for the way we ... intruded on you yesterday," Sarah's mother said to Winston. "And then the way we reacted was not perhaps ideal. I said the same to Kirsten, but I don't think she was in the mood to hear it."

"Oh, so Winston gets an apology."

"Hey, whose life is ruined here exactly? You get to be the big doctor that Mom and Dad brag about, and you have a boyfriend who used to be my best friend."

Jake said, "I'm not a Matchbox car, Winston. Sarah didn't exactly steal me and put me in her toy box."

"Enough," thundered Mr. Soon.

Even he looked kind of impressed by how loud he managed to be. But he made a quick recovery. "Obviously, we have mismanaged some things."

"That's a way of putting it. You missed your calling as a corporate lawyer, Pa."

"Don't heckle Dad, Sarah."

"Why don't you go chase your girlfriend for another couple of miles, Winston?"

"You—you have no right to talk to me after what you did. You walloped me in the face. I should press charges! I should sue. Then you humiliated me by running after me around the room and throwing food at me. Who does that?"

"You've been nothing but a surly asshole to me since you arrived—actually, since birth. And the way you treat your girlfriend—not even just doing basic things like getting her some coffee when she had to wake up in a strange house or, I don't know, introducing her to Mom and Dad instead of just sneaking her into your hotel room. And why the hell didn't you just answer a damn text and save yourself the trouble, you amateur? And how about standing up to Mom and Dad for her when they were weird to her last night? Let's just say maybe your behavior had something to do with the fact that she dumped you."

Winston gasped in outrage. He turned to his mom.

Things seemed to be getting out of control again.

"Maybe we should all sit down instead of standing around yelling at each other," Jake suggested wearily.

"Since when does *he* get to stay?"

"Since he's the only one who isn't acting like a child," Mrs. Soon muttered.

But she sat. And everyone else followed suit.

"I guess we're having it out, then," Sarah said, squaring her shoulders.

She looked ready for a fight, not for reconciliation. But then, even sitting, none of them seemed very ready to move in the direction of hugs and jokes. Despite Sarah's tough stance, she also looked on the verge of tears.

Jake wanted to take her hand. But he didn't. He was still absorbing what she had said about him so long ago. He reminded himself that they had both been different people then. Still, the words had surprised him, and he found he was wary. The sooner he got the family to talk, the sooner he'd have a chance to hash it out with Sarah. But even he was losing his patience.

Mr. Soon, seemingly unaware of the tensions that were already heavy in the air, cleared his throat. "So, your mother and I have been concerned for a while about our relationships with you.

Things seem strained and … perhaps you have not always been forthright when it comes to things like"—he motioned at Jake—"boyfriends and girlfriends."

"Or your health," Sarah's mom added.

"We're asking for understanding. And maybe that you come see us more often. And tell us about your life. I don't really want things to continue down this path. I realize that will take some work on our part, but, uh, the one thing that you can say about us is that we've never been afraid of work."

Sarah was shaking her head. "I don't know if I'm going to be able to do that.

Despite all that had happened between them, Jake's heart squeezed. Sarah was looking torn. But strong. She didn't want to give up that righteous anger that had kept her focused and together for such a long time. Maybe her parents' rejection of her in those last awful months of high school had been terrible, but she'd made herself what she was, and she was amazing now.

Maybe he could do the same with all that Winston had said this morning. The hurt lingered. It stirred up old feelings that he thought he'd forgotten. But people could change—they had to. It was something he had to believe because of his profession—that the right interventions at the right moments could alter lives. But all of those adjustments and modifications were work. And at the same time, he had to be wary of people who claimed too readily that they had turned over a new leaf—those abusive boyfriends and parents, people who promised too much too easily.

Well, none of the Soons had been easy. He watched Sarah's face—so young and raw in its anger. Her change was hard earned. Was she still that scornful golden girl? No, not entirely. Did a part of her still see him as an awkward, dorky do-gooder who had abandoned her? Well, a part of him was still that person. But what he had to get over was his own teenage feeling that someone like her would be interested in someone like him. It wasn't that he had to accept Sarah had changed—it was that he had to have faith that he was now different, too. He was better than that stupid kid he had been. And after all, wasn't the fact that she wanted him here with her proof that she believed in the person he had become?

"So that's it, huh?" Sarah continued. "We're another one of your projects. Made a mess with the kids, try to salvage it for parts before it goes to waste."

"Sarah."

"You came here to my house. You summoned Winston for some sort of family reconciliation vacation. And you expect us all to hug and make up? Mom, Dad, I thought you guys were realists. Because one chat like this isn't going to make me trust you."

"Oh, get over it," Winston interjected. "All the bad crap went down, like, fifteen years ago, and you're still holding it over all our heads."

"I'm still holding onto it? Winston? You're the one who just hurt your best friend over the incredibly stupid remarks that I made even longer ago."

"Don't shift the blame to me."

"I'm not. I was terrible to you and to Jake, and I'm sorry. But telling *me* to get over it when you clearly, clearly are never going to let it go? Maybe I don't want to get over it. Maybe *I* should never get over it, because I have made something of myself because of it. I should really thank you all for showing me that *I don't need you. I am fine on my own. I don't need anyone."

She reached out to grasp Jake's hand as she said it. It was a half apology buried in defiance. He didn't know how to feel about it. And the rest of it was true; Sarah didn't need anyone—not her family, and maybe not him. He'd even said it—several times—but this was the first time that it hit him quite this way. He protected people—had built an entire career around it. He'd broken up his marriage because he was no longer what his wife needed—and she wasn't what he needed. But here was Sarah, self sufficient and strong. She didn't depend on him to swoop in and fix things. It was terrifying how much *he* needed her. She could be strong, and she could comfort him. But what was he going to be to her?

He would not accept being an afterthought.

She was still talking though. "In fact, I can't see why this is happening right now. I don't see why you're here to fix your loose ends unless someone's dying."

She stopped in the silence. Even Winston looked shocked. "Wait, is one of you ill? Are you dying?"

Fai said, "Well, you almost did, Sarah. You almost did, and you didn't tell us."

Another pause. Then Sarah got up. "You don't get to use me."

"We're not—"

Jake got up. Sarah said, "I'm sorry, Jake. I'm so sorry. I can't deal with this now."

And she ran.

• • •

Her family felt guilty. Well, good. They should.

They had no right. Her illness was hers. Her recovery was hers. And her relationships and her life were hers, and their sudden show of feeling was too confusing.

The only person who hadn't muddled her was Jake. She'd said she didn't need anyone, but he had held her hand. He'd accepted her grasp even though she had been hateful to him so long ago.

Sarah wanted to go back for him, but she had jumped on her rarely used bike (she really needed to practice more if she wanted to do the Big Eastside Trail Loop). Here she was without a helmet! Without sunscreen! She could be reckless and stupid, and she was pedaling away as fast as she could, as if she had no power to interrupt her momentum.

She reached the park and got off to walk the bike. And she just folded, collapsing onto the grass. She was staring at the sun—another thing that she shouldn't do. Today was just full of things to cross off the list, wasn't it?

A dog snuffled up to her and her licked her face.

"Oh wow, I'm so sorry. He's not usually that forward," a voice said.

The man attached to the voice didn't look that sorry, though, as Sarah sat up. He was objectively handsome, and he knew it. Not as nearly as good as Jake, though, who was all the more attractive because he wasn't drenched in the stench of presumption.

The stranger stretched, a preening gesture, and motioned beside her. "Mind if I sit down?"

Without waiting for an answer, he collapsed into the grass next to her and edged a little too close.

Maybe at some distant point in the past, she would have been flattered by his attention. But she'd just had an emotional shouting match with her family. She was clearly upset and attempting to think, and all this man was doing was buzzing around, trying to make her focus on him instead of her own thoughts.

Jake had not done that. He could have caused a scene. He could have yelled at her. She thought of the million things and ways he could have made himself the center of attention. But he'd waited for her.

And she had run out on him.

She'd thought she had to resolve things with her parents in order to be happy in love. It had always been in the back of her mind. After she'd confronted them with how terrible they'd been and they said they were sorry, after they'd changed themselves into completely different people, *then* she could try to have a good relationship with someone. That's what she'd been telling herself.

But she'd already found the person she wanted, and she shouldn't—couldn't—make him wait any more.

She wanted Jake right now. She needed to hear him. She loved his reasonable tone, his crinkly-eyed smile. She missed him when he wasn't around. No, she did not require his presence in order to make every decision—and no, she did not need him in order to be able to survive and stand on her own two feet. But she needed more than that; her happiness was worth a lot more than that. Her parents wanted to try to be in her life again. Her brother—maybe not so much—but maybe it didn't matter. She deserved someone who would care for her the way Jake did—the way he had proven again and again—and she deserved to love him back. He knew her at her very worst—crusted in porridge, screaming at her family—and he loved her. He had not backed down or run away—not the way she had just now.

Things didn't have to be perfect for her to move forward with her life.

If nothing else came of this terrible morning, it was this realization. And now she'd figured out this one thing. She loved him and she always would.

She didn't want to waste any more time.

She interrupted her admirer. "*Actually*, I was just leaving."

She sprang up grabbed her bike.

"Hey, was it something I said?"

"Not everything is about you, dude."

She pedaled home as quickly as she could, determined to figure something out with Jake. She wasn't sure what, but she was sure he had a lot of suggestions. Maybe a list. But as she reached her sidewalk, she saw Jake outside. Was he preparing to leave?

"Jake!"

His face turned, and she saw the relief and love in it. She called his name again and zoomed her bike into the walk as her parents' car shot out, tail first.

Then there was a horrible jolt, a thud, and surprise. There was noise—and so much bewildering pain.

The last distinct thing she heard was Winston screaming, "I'm so sorry. Oh no, I'm so sorry."

• • •

Jake knew the protocol. The family would get to see her first. Even fucking Winston could be allowed in the room before him.

None of this should matter as long as she was all right—but it did. He was going to tell her he loved her again. He was going to say that he'd wait for her to make up her mind, that he wasn't going to rush her, but that she would to have to let him try and convince her that he needed her, selfishly and unreservedly, and that she was going to have to live with that.

He would fight to get in that room first—because this was important.

Sarah's friend Helen was the one to come out to speak to them. "She's broken her left wrist and some ribs, but she'll be all right."

Jake let out a breath of relief. "I'm going to see her *now*."

The rest of the family stood, but Jake had been too keyed up for too long to tolerate their presence any longer. He spun around and stared them down. "You've had your turn," he told Sarah's family.

Helen agreed with him. She glared at the Soons over his shoulder, then transferred her gaze to Jake. "You were her first thought," she told him. "The rest of you can wait back here."

Helen gave Winston an especially hard stare. "She wanted to get out of bed to make sure that I came to get you—and only you," Helen murmured to Jake before turning to usher him to the room.

Sarah did look like she was ready for a fight despite her pallor. Her dark hair was loose and wild, and her mouth was stretched in a tight line of pain, but her eyes were trained anxiously at the door. When she saw him, her face glowed with relief and something more.

Despite the cast on her wrist, she opened her arms, and he held her as fiercely and as gingerly as he could.

"It's you," she said.

"Couldn't keep me away."

"I really hope," she said, her voice muffled, "that every time I realize something important I won't wind up in a hospital bed."

"You're going to tire yourself out."

"No. I'm not. I want to say I'm sorry. Apologizing to you was the first thing I should have done. I should never have agreed with my friends all those years ago."

Jake wanted to laugh. "I don't care."

"But I gave you such a hard time when we met up again."

"The situations were different. Plus, we had old ideas about each other that needed clearing up—and they were cleared up. I just want you to be better now."

"I promise you, I'll get better and I'll do better. Just like you've been doing with your entire life."

They didn't speak again for a while. It was good to sit silently and absorb the warmth of each other.

Sarah gave a small sudden laugh, her breath tickling his ear. It was the best feeling in the world. "I was being too quiet at first, so Helen pushed the resident out of the way and checked me another two times."

"Maybe she should go for a third."

"Would you still love me if I did injure my head and had no short term memory and got a huge scar across my forehead?"

He pulled back and touched her bruised cheek gently. "Is this something you're planning? Because I don't see that scar yet. To tell you the truth, I don't know if I'm quite ready to joke about this yet. Seeing the car hit you—seeing you bleeding on the ground—that was the single worst moment of my life."

Sarah gave a watery laugh. "Well, that's saying something, because the last year has been pretty full of bad moments for you."

He shook his head. "And good ones. Seeing you again, being with you, arguing with you, being in bed with you, and waking up with you have all been the happiest times of my life."

He didn't want to let go of her. That was all he knew. And she didn't seem to want to let go of him.

But her face clouded slightly. "I left you sad and doubting last night and this morning. I couldn't stop myself from doing the things I always do, having the same arguments."

"I know you love me."

"But I should have sought you out first and apologized and reassured you."

"I wish you had, too, at the time. But I understand. Sarah, I'll support whatever relationship you want or don't want with your family. But just don't let it dictate your actions. Don't let them have this power."

She closed her eyes and nodded. "It's going to be hard to get out of that habit, but you're right. And I don't know what kind of relationship we'll have moving forward. But one thing I do know, you are the one for me, Jake."

She was looking at him now, her face glowing with love. "I know I go for some dubious self-improvement schemes and that I'm stubborn and angry. But *you* are the one who makes my life better. You listen and you laugh with me, and you see me and you respond. You're the one who takes what I already am and makes it richer. I'm not ready to get married or have kids or any of that kind of thing just right now—I feel like I have to figure out my life again because of everything that's happened—but one thing I do know is that I need you in my life. It's the only thing that has stood out clearly to me. Never doubt that I'm committed to you, that I want to be holding your hand, or walking the dog with you, or just riding in the car talking and not talking. You are what I want."

"That is exactly what I needed to hear." He added very seriously, "I was pushing too fast. But it's because I want time with you, because all of that time is a pleasure. It doesn't matter what name we give it."

She grimaced. "This isn't the most romantic setting for my declaration. And I'm not exactly in the best shape to celebrate."

"The best stuff is always overrated."

"I had more that I was going to say to you. And now I can't even remember."

"It'll keep."

CHAPTER TWENTY-TWO

It was a gorgeous weekend for a wedding.

There was a lot Sarah had forgotten about her hometown. That it was beautiful in fall with bright leaves everywhere, and that it smelled good—that the scent of rain was extra fresh and invigorating on the drive through the countryside.

Laketon had changed; there was no doubt about that. There was indeed a yoga and Pilates studio and a new outdoor adventure store with bikes and hiking gear. The diner was still there with Georgie behind the counter, but the sign was new, hand painted. And the cracked brown leather of the booths had been swapped out with a bright red. And there were green juices on the menu.

Sarah was slightly annoyed by it, in truth. Between sips of a Kale-ing Me Softly With Beet Juice, she groused good-naturedly with Jake about hipsters and hippies and what this town was coming to. Every now and then, an old classmate of theirs, or a friend of their parents stopped by their booth and said hello and congratulations.

She wouldn't say she was completely mollified by the welcome. Then again, she had a full and rich life elsewhere. It didn't matter as much anymore what people said and thought.

After checking in to their room at the new inn and changing into their finery, they drove to the reverend's house and picked him up to take him to his wedding. The Catholic priest and Baptist minister and their new buddy from the Sikh temple shared the honors in marrying Reverend Doctor Telly Li to Dr. Judy Yu-san

Tai. The crowd broke out into applause, and the dancing lasted well past midnight.

Jake was the best man. He wore a dark blue suit with a subtle sheen to it, and Sarah had very unholy thoughts during the simple ceremony at the big church.

The reception was large and loud and crowded. Judy had waited a long time for a wedding, and the reverend wanted to give her a blowout celebration—also, he liked parties. The reverend had lived in Laketon for more than thirty years. He'd invited the whole town and his whole congregation. Sarah's mom had organized it, and she spent most of the night in an electric blue dress directing traffic at the buffet tables and re-arranging the torchlights. She was in her element.

Sarah and Jake danced for a long time under the stars and pointed out the constellations to each other. After toasts and cake, they went back to the inn, peeled their clothes off, and sauntered into in the room-sized shower. And because they were grown-ups, they could turn on the various showerheads whenever they wanted—even if it was after midnight—and have slippery sex against the wall or on the floor. Sarah had to admit that the new inn was very, very well equipped.

Jake got up and shut off the taps. He pulled her up into a warm towel and dried her hair and took her back to the bed and rubbed her carefully.

"Thank you. My tits and ass are very dry," Sarah said.

She was sleepy. But her eye did pop open when Jake kneeled on the floor in front of her. "Don't worry, I'm not going to make any rash declarations," he said.

It was a standing joke between them now. He'd come back from a run smelling like grass and sweat and rain and kiss her and say, "Don't worry, I'm not going make a declaration."

But she wasn't thinking of much at all. Especially when he lifted her legs up and tucked her firmly into the bed and then burrowed under the covers with her, pulling her to his warm, naked body.

"What's going through your mind?" he asked, tracing her ear.

"I'm trying not to mind the visit to my parents tomorrow. I mean, be prepared for them to be snippy about the fact that we didn't stay with them."

"Sounds great."

"And for them to bust our chops about the grandchildren they want."

He put his nose in her neck, and she knew he was taking in a deep calming lungful of the scent of her soap.

"They're trying," she said. "But they forget themselves."

"Then I will very wisely get us to leave when they start in on it."

"They have good intentions. But it's going to take them a while to change. Good thing they like improvement projects."

He laughed against her neck, and it tickled. "Oh, I heard from Winston. He's been working on it, but he got back together with Kirsten after many apologies and promises to be less of an asshole. I think hitting you with his car scared him into being a better person."

"I'm glad my incapacitation achieved something."

"Well, speaking of bed rest, I plan to keep you here for a scandalously long time this weekend."

"Past 9:00 a.m.?"

"Maybe till ten or eleven. We're going to have to get lots of rest, especially now that you'll start delivering midnight babies again soon."

"And yet something tells me you don't have sleep in mind."

"Just building up your tolerance for long, long hours."

"You're such a giver."

She hit him with a pillow, and the ensuing battle was epic and glorious. She was Sarah Soon, maker of lists, taker of names, kicker of asses, and she was happy.

Acknowledgments

I am proud and fortunate to work with the glorious team at Crimson; Jessica Verdi, Tara Gelsomino, and Julie Sturgeon have guided me gently but firmly through three books, and I would be nowhere without them.

Many thanks to Amber Belldene, who was there with encouragement, advice, and a compassionate eye. To my husband, thank you for listening to my ranting and whining, and for pointing out my overuse of em-dashes.

Finally Toasties and SpaceWitches, to quote the great Sophia Loren, "Everything you see I owe to pasta." Except, my darlings, *the pasta is you.*

About the Author

Ruby Lang is pint-sized, prim, and bespectacled. Her alter ego, essayist Mindy Hung, has written for *The New York Times*, *The Toast*, and *Salon* among others. She enjoys running (slowly), reading (quickly), and ice cream (at any speed). She lives in New York with a small child and a medium-sized husband.

More from This Author

Hard Knocks

Ruby Lang

What a day for seeing the sights, Helen Chang Frobisher thought as she entered the exam room and took in the two mountain ranges facing her.

In the chair: the Alps. On the table: the Andes.

Of course, Portland never lacked for scenic views, but the two physically imposing gentlemen in front of her were a different story. They turned their boulder-hewn faces toward her and squared their chiseled shoulders. Alps stood up, but Andes just closed his eyes again. Clearly, he was her man.

Lacerations to the forehead and scalp, her brain noted as her heels clicked forward.

Andes was in a hospital gown. Alps was wearing a nattily tailored suit, but she doubted he was a businessman. Both men were too large, too craggy, too ... panoramic, she thought briefly before putting on her doctor face.

They had been sewn up. The chart indicated minor contusions on the blond one she'd dubbed Alps. Dark-haired and dark-eyed Andes, however, had clearly taken a harder hit.

"Dr. Frobisher, I thought you'd be interested in meeting these gentlemen," Dr. Max Weber yelped. He flapped his clipboard excitedly.

She hadn't even noticed her colleague next to the huge men, so preoccupied she had been. He was practically dancing.

"Their minor car accident is our special treat!" Weber said. "Dr. Frobisher, I'd like you to meet—but wait, you probably already know who they are."

Max looked eagerly at Helen. Blond Alps, the one who wasn't white-faced in the bed, came slowly toward her. She looked way, way up into his eyes. Smarter than the average landmass, she thought, meeting his alert, interested gaze. He cleared his throat. "Dr. Frobisher," he said, "I'm Adam Magnus and that lump over there is Serge Beaufort."

He put out his hand, and she took it, her slender fingers immediately lost in his palm. Out of sheer bloody-mindedness, she was tempted to squeeze with everything she had. She took in his close-cropped blond hair and the Slavic cheekbones. His eyes were that color that everyone said was blue, but which she privately thought of as ghostly and white. But there was a disarming sprinkling of freckles across his nose—a nose that had been broken once or twice. *Farm boy meets gladiator*, she thought, trying once more to fit him into neat categories.

She caught another glimmer of amusement from him and ignored it.

A nurse had wrapped a bandage around Alps's forehead—Adam Magnus's, she corrected herself—and there was a little blood on his shirt. Minor head wounds had a tendency to bleed a lot. Still, what the hell was wrong with her colleague, Weber? He was fluttering around the patients like a drunken Southern belle. She flicked her gaze back at Magnus.

"You should probably sit down, Mr. Magnus," she told him.

"I'm fine," he said. He was still holding her hand. "Dr. Weber and the nurses in the ER already worked their magic."

"Dr. Frobisher," Max screeched, "you don't know who these gentlemen are? Serge Beaufort is the goalie of the Oregon Wolves, and Adam Magnus here is the enforcer. He's the guy who makes sure everyone stays clear of our other players."

"That's great," said Helen extricating her hand. She moved closer to Andes. She still wasn't sure why she was here. Maybe something had shown up on a CT scan. "And the Wolves are ..."

"They're our hockey team."

"Portland has a hockey team? No offense," she added, with a quick grin to the patients.

Andes barely registered her words. Alps quirked her a wry smile.

Helen felt her stomach tighten a fraction.

Adam Magnus was kind of gorgeous, if you went for the gigantic, lethal bodyguard look.

Helen didn't.

Well, not usually.

Weber was offended for the players' sakes. "Are you telling me you don't follow hockey? Doesn't anyone watch the Wolves in this town? Helen, you're Canadian, for God's sake."

"I don't follow hockey nowadays," Helen said, shrugging. "So ... no one here is complaining of chronic headache, I take it."

She turned to the patient with a barely suppressed sigh. Head trauma was not her specialty—she usually looked at migraine and pain, but Weber had called her in on a routine mild traumatic brain injury case just because he thought she'd like to meet some hockey players. She supposed she ought to be grateful that her supervisor was the enthusiastic sort who paid attention to his charges.

Weber gestured for Helen to check the patient out. She ran through her list of standard questions, observing her patient's hearing, his speech, his memory. *Definitely a concussion*, she thought, as she wound down her exam. Interestingly, Beaufort's coordination and reflexes were still quite sharp.

Athletes, she thought again.

They'd probably both been playing since they were barely old enough to skate. That was how they honed that coordination and those reflexes that could grab bullets out of the air. That was how they learned the stick was an extension of their limbs. The movements were practiced and repeated and practiced until the procedures of each specific motor task, each grip on the stick, each flick of the wrist, each turn of the head, became etched in the neuroanatomy. Her brother had played for a while. Fat lot of good that had done him.

She quickly checked off another set of boxes in her head as she completed Serge Beaufort's exam. He was murmuring in French, something about a puppy.

Oh, she was just enough of a snob to think that all those beautiful masculine reflexes could be put to something more interesting: ice sculpting, puppeteering, exotic dancing, Swedish massage. But instead, they chose to chase a little round pellet around the ice while wearing helmets and loose jerseys. It seemed like such a waste of flesh. She'd read a study that looked at whether athletes had a limited range of facial and vocal expressions because most of their concentration had gone into developing their larger muscle groups. She peered at Serge Beaufort's slack jaw again. His eyes were closed.

Unfair to judge the poor man right now, she thought. He had, after all, suffered a blow to the head.

But the mountain behind her, Adam Magnus, he had an imperturbable athlete's face. She sneaked a peek at him. No, that wasn't quite true. From a distance, he seemed impassive, but up close, he was hardly vacant. There was a restlessness around his eyes and mouth. His voice, although not animated, was deep and amused. So he chose to work in a profession where he used his body more than his brain. No wonder he had a smile in his voice. She'd cackle if she were paid handsomely to fill out designer suits and hit pucks. His buddies probably thought it was fine for him to gun his sports car on a Sunday afternoon and get into traffic accidents. They probably jeered whenever he punched someone, guffawed when he kneed someone in the groin.

There. She'd put Adam Magnus in his box and shut the lid.

God, she was a horrible, judgmental shrew these days. How the hell was she supposed to be a good doctor if she was already this cynical at the beginning of her career?

She finished up her notes on Serge Beaufort, aware of Adam's eyes on her. It was almost as if he could hear her thoughts. She felt herself redden, just a little, so she tightened her face and held her spine straight even as a small part of her failed.

It was this way all the time, now. She was angry, easily frazzled. She lost her concentration. If she kept this up, she'd be useless to her patients. There was no need to resent Adam Magnus. There was no need to be spiteful with everyone and anyone for simply being.

Except, she was.

Nurse Pham came in with the CT scan, and Weber left with her, chattering the whole time.

Helen took a deep breath. Her life was not terrible. Actually, it had been pretty charmed. Small-town upbringing in the Okanagan Valley, daughter of one of the town doctors, a house with dogs, wide-plank tables, and sunshine. She'd picked apples and done ballet. She had an older brother to assume the burden of being a perfect child. And she had been so stupid, so gloriously stupid, to take that for granted, to think that the whole thing would be forever preserved in the honey of memory, that her parents would always be fortyish, strong and wise and healthy, and that she would always return to find things that way.

She'd spent a few unhappy years in her teens at the San Francisco Ballet School, but that home—that beautiful home nestled in Canada—was the constant. When she finally quit dancing, college and medical school and residency went by in a whirl of work and studying and trying to sleep.

Everything until then had been good. Then her father's diagnosis came, just a couple of months after she'd started practicing as a neurologist. He'd been a boxer in his youth, and he'd suffered minor head trauma from a car accident a few months prior to diagnosis. But no one could say if either was linked to his growing illness, and it wasn't much use trying to find out. She'd handled that well at first, too. She'd conferred with her dad's physicians when she'd flown up to see her parents. Degenerative brain disease wasn't her specialty, but she'd researched treatments and gone about her life with the usual practical optimism that one expected from a doctor. Except that he'd only gotten worse. And now she could say that all her optimism was gone.

She was grateful that this patient was disoriented, so that he couldn't gauge how far her mind wandered during this exam.

She pocketed her pen and tried to smooth down the ridges of her sudden anger.

"How is he?" asked Adam Magnus.

His voice was unexpectedly close to her ear.

"We'll keep him overnight for observation," she told him.

"We have an away game tomorrow."

She wanted to flip him the bird.

"Dr. Weber will confer with your team physician," she said crisply. "But the fact is, Mr. Beaufort has had a concussion. He needs to rest, and air travel would exacerbate his condition."

He was only looking out for his friend's job, she told herself. No need think the worst of him.

"Your turn," she said. "Sit down."

She should just go on her way, she thought. But for some reason, she needed to establish some sort of authority over him. And he did indeed have a head injury, minor though it was, and head injuries interested her.

"I've already been checked," he protested.

"Scientific curiosity. This isn't really an exam," she said, giving his sturdy chest a little push. "And you're not my patient, and I'm not really your doctor. Just call it an opinion."

"I guess some opinions are stronger than others," he said, with that glint again.

Mercilessly, she shone her penlight right into his laughing eyes. His pupils constricted immediately.

She went through the motions of an exam, but there didn't seem to be much to see, *just as he had pointed out*, she told herself. Alps was fine. More than fine. Sure, he had a few nicks and dents, but he was still solid and golden. She felt a little foolish for pushing him around, making him sit. She had just wanted to put him in a separate place, but it hadn't worked. For some reason, he made her jumpy. She felt transparent. She had needed to put him where he couldn't touch her, and now she was the one touching him.

She moved her hand away.

His phone trilled with an irritating, old-fashioned telephone ring, and he glanced at her apologetically.

"You're fine," she said curtly. "I'll get a nurse in to finish up with your friend."

She turned on her heel, and Adam stood with his back to her as he talked quietly on the phone.

She closed the door and walked down the hallway to give Weber the lowdown. She checked in with Nurse Pham and signed her forms. The hockey players had been the last of her patients. She was off the clock. Now would be a perfect time to call her mother. She hiked over to the physicians' lounge.

"It's your dad's naptime," May Yin Frobisher said over the phone. "I hate to wake him when it's so hard to get him to sleep."

Helen knew it was. It was why she had chosen to call now instead of later. She squelched down her guilt and became brisk. "Just a quick check-in today. How is his depression?" she asked. "How is the new medication working out for him?"

She and her mother ran through their set list of questions. While they talked, it was easy to forget that this was her mother and that the patient with parkinsonism was her own father.

Satisfied, she was about to hang up, when May Yin said, hesitantly, "Helen, I've been thinking. With your dad's condition being the way it is, we'd like to move to a smaller place. Somewhere without stairs."

"Mum, Dad's doing fine right now. The new medication has been working well. The tremors are under control."

May Yin was silent. She was probably twisting her still-black hair. Her husband and daughter often ganged up to veto her. It never did any good, Helen thought with a sick twist in her stomach. Besides, with her father deteriorating every day, he didn't have a say.

When May Yin spoke again, her voice had become precise and distant. "It would be better for us to move before your father gets worse—"

Helen wanted to open her mouth, but May Yin kept talking, ruthlessly and without inflection. "It is only going to go downhill from here," she said. "I've been asking your brother to look for condos in Vancouver, so that we'll be near him and Gordon, closer to the kinds of medical services that your father needs. Helen, I know it's your childhood home and you love it, but I can't do this anymore. I can't take care of your father by myself. I can't drive hours every week to take him to specialists. I can't pick up after him and cook and keep the house clean—"

"I'll send you money for a housekeeper. And you can hire someone to drive you."

She grimaced as she heard herself. This was exactly the kind of illogic she discouraged in patients and families. And here she was thinking magically, *If I don't go back, my father won't worsen. He'll stay the way I left him. The house will be perfect and welcoming. Everything will be okay.*

She closed her eyes and wished her words back, but her mother, who had a lot to deal with these days, had a short fuse, too. "I know this upsets you, Helen. But I've already made a decision. Besides, if we move, it'll make it easier for you to visit."

May Yin hung up.

Her mother was quietly angry, which Helen was used to. She could hardly blame her mother. Helen had not been to see her parents since summer. She didn't live that far down the coast from them. And added to the fact that she and her father had always been close, she was a neurologist. She could be of use to him.

Except when she couldn't.

She shoved the phone back in her pocket and strode out of the room as if she knew where she was going.

Her father's central nervous system was failing. His brain was shutting down and dying, and here she was with her fancy medical degree, and there was not a thing she could do about it.

•••

Adam could not afford to be distracted, least of all by the woman who had just left the room. But her gestures had been so deft, her movements so precise—it was fascinating to watch her, and much more pleasant than the task at hand.

He was dimly aware that the first doctor—Weber, his name was—had come back in and was reassuring him about Serge's health. Of course Serge would be fine. He'd taken worse hits before. But the media attention for this traffic accident was probably going to be ugly, even though the kid was fine. The season had barely started, and the Wolves were already in a losing streak. Worse, this was only the team's second year in operation, but already it was their second year occupying the bottom of the NHL rankings. The town was indifferent to the team unless the players did something stupid. Their billionaire owner was reviled.

Hardly anyone showed up to games. Hell, they hadn't even been able to get crowds into the goodwill pancake breakfast they'd held.

And then there was the arena.

The stupid fucking arena.

They needed all the positive publicity they could get. Two team members getting into a car accident with a seventeen-year-old girl would not make for pretty headlines: *Teenager. Accident. Hockey Goons.* Bad optics, someone might say, even though Adam hadn't been drinking or speeding or doing anything reckless. They'd been coming back from a Sunday afternoon benefit for a sports camp when the girl had run a red light and plowed into them. Luckily, the kid was fine, if a little shaken up. Adam felt sorry for her. But now Serge and Adam had a light shining on them, just when it was best to lie low.

Adam already left a message with his and Serge's manager. No doubt the team's GM would be alerted soon enough, as would the media. Adam winced. Some Norwegian player they'd brought in to replace the kid from Duluth had been fired last week. A rookie from Ontario had been dropped two weeks ago. The team was playing badly. Everyone was hanging on to their jobs by a thread. All it took was this kind of thing for someone to find an excuse to can Adam too.

It had taken seven years, but he was now a realist about his career; he wasn't much longer for this gig. If he had been a better player on a better team, he might have looked forward to a career in coaching, or maybe he could become a sportscaster, run a themed bar with decent memorabilia and Guinness on tap. Maybe he could have started a camp. But he wasn't particularly gifted as a player—not like some of the other guys on the Wolves' roster who might have thrived in a different environment. Adam hadn't scored all season and was unlikely to in future. He was the muscle. Muscle was abundant and cheap. It didn't last.

He blew out a frustrated sigh.

Dr. Weber was now offering tips for how to improve his game. Adam gave him a weak thumbs up. He should be considering his survival strategy. He should be totting up his finances, sweeping the supermarket for dented cans of soup, and making damn sure he could afford to live over the next few years.

But a good part of his mind was preoccupied with Helen Frobisher, neurologist.

She was pretty, in a sober, sheltered, breakable way. Brown hair—not chestnut, not auburn. *Brown.* And in a ridiculously tight bun. No makeup. She had delicate ears, a graceful neck, a long thin nose with a slight bump in it, and thin lips, which made her look fastidious and intellectual. Her skin had an olive cast, and yet, it still looked like she spent a lot of time indoors, peering at CAT scans, probably, or mixing up mystery formulas. She seemed delicate from far away. But that wasn't what had made him notice her.

After a moment talking to her, looking at her, he'd realized it would be a mistake to think of her as fragile. Her posture was perfect. She spoke crisply, and her eyes were ever alert. It was her hands that really captured him. There was no way she was any sort of weakling, not with such strong, deft hands, which sliced through the air quickly and ruthlessly. The movements of fingers and palm were controlled, but they spoke. *Expressive*, he thought. *Angry.* That was a little surprising. When the gloves came off, guys he'd met on the ice who had less aggression in their fists than Dr. Helen Frobisher.

He wondered what had set her off, and as he'd watched more closely, he grew more conscious of the movement of fine muscles under the arms and shoulders of her white coat. He had learned some things about how people moved, and—well—it was a pleasure to watch her. He had found himself moving closer just to observe. Of course, that had gotten her hackles up, until she pushed him into a chair to make him behave.

And he had liked that last part. A lot.

It was funny. People prodded Adam all the time. Trainers, physios, masseurs, teammates, opponents were always poking him, punching, or grabbing his arms, looking at bumps, positioning his limbs and torso. There was always a physician checking his knees, his arms, his hips, a coach eyeing his hands and legs. His body was not his own. But he'd never been examined quite this way by a steely, young woman. When she shone a flashlight in his eyes and started firing questions at him, he felt his skin and guts jump to her commands.

She was compelling. *Formidable.* She was a long line of adjectives fit for an army general. She'd made him focus almost as if she were an opponent, someone facing him on the ice. Her serious, fine-boned face, her sharpness, it was all completely new for him. She made him feel alert, he thought, a little surprised; it hadn't occurred to him that he had been going through the motions lately.

More interesting, she'd clearly reacted to him too. She bristled when he drew near. Sure, her tone seemed even and deliberately mild, her face controlled. But he wondered if she had any idea how vivid her hands were. From the white doctor's coat, her wrists emerged as fragile as a paper crane until they tightened around a pen or sliced through the air to illustrate her thoughts. And then those sinews and bones flexed, and she flashed her penlight right into his eyes like she wished it were a dagger.

He had admired it all way too much.

He had also enjoyed the way she'd needed to stand very close to him, too. One huge brown eye had been practically in his. If she'd tilted her head and he'd bent his and she moved a fraction of an inch sideways, they would have been lip to lip, teeth to teeth, tongue pressed to tongue. Luckily, she pulled back for a minute, and because it was right there, he looked past the curve of her neck and right down her blouse. Sky-blue bra, he noted dizzily.

The sight of her skin peeking through fabric and lace would be imprinted in his brain. *Not cool, Magnus,* he had told himself, looking away. Not cool at all.

He blinked himself back to the present, thanked Dr. Weber, then went back to the hallway to call Bobby, his manager, again.

Bobby jabbered worriedly.

Adam said, "No, we weren't drinking at all. Girl plowed through a stoplight and right into us. Serge is out of tomorrow's game."

Bobby wasn't the sharpest manager, but then, Adam wasn't the best player. He and Serge were Bobby's two major clients. He had signed them both years ago, back when their bones were more or less intact and their futures had looked sunny. The rest of Bobby's roster comprised softball players, lesser American marathoners, and a couple of minor league pitchers. He wasn't a shark. Bobby was more of a clownfish, darting in and out and feeding off of the scraps.

Adam being a scrap.

He paced the hospital hallway and tried to concentrate. "Look," he said. "I'm fine. I'm being discharged. Just tell me where they want me to be and what they want me to say, and I'll do it. But Serge is pretty banged up, and he isn't going anywhere."

Within minutes, text instructions began arriving. Adam said good-bye to a sleeping Serge, signed his discharge papers, and looked around for Helen Frobisher.

She strode past him and gave him a short nod. But her eyes looked sad. Never mind. He would never see this woman again.

He took a cab back to the team's offices. He had to admit, the management team was better at crisis than the players were at playing. They'd had more practice. He changed his shirt and went up to the press center. A few people briefed him, but he knew the drill: Say as little as possible, look blank and bland. He would sit beside Coach and answer questions monosyllabically, with long pauses in between words. There was no need to talk about Serge's condition. After less than an hour, they threw the doors open to face the bloggers and writers and sportscasters. After a moment of silence, the management team's faces fell.

Not one reporter had bothered to come.

For more from Ruby Lang, check out:
Acute Reactions
Praise for Ruby Lang:

"Lang writes funny, feisty, and quirky characters finding love in all the wrong places."—Alyssa Cole for *Culturess*

"From a protagonist who can never find her car to sentences rich with subtle humor, Lang's witty voice gives this novel its charm."—*RT Book Reviews*

"This is a cute story with convincing characters! Each one has some kind of ethical baggage, which makes for some thought-provoking interactions between them all."—4.5 stars, *InD'tale Magazine*

"What a cute book. Smart, funny, and good banter. Some of my favorite things." —*Smexy Books*

"Ruby Lang just landed on my auto-buy list." —*Cooking Up Romance*

"A charming, funny, and deeply emotional romance" —*Immersed in Books*

In the mood for more Crimson Romance?
Check out *The Sweet Spot by Elley Arden*
at CrimsonRomance.com.

Printed in the United States
By Bookmasters